The Secret of the Seven Willows

For Erica—
To a great kid!

Thomas McKean

The Secret of the Seven Willows

Thomas McKean

HALF MOON BOOKS

Published by Simon & Schuster

New York · London · Toronto · Sydney · Tokyo · Singapore

HALF MOON BOOKS
Simon & Schuster Building, Rockefeller Center
1230 Avenue of the Americas, New York, New York 10020

Designed by Lucille Chomowicz
Also available in a SIMON & SCHUSTER BOOKS
FOR YOUNG READERS hardcover edition.
Manufactured in the United States of America   10   9   8   7   6   5   4   3   2   1

Library of Congress Cataloging-in-Publication Data: McKean, Thomas.
Secret of the seven willows/by Thomas McKean. (Doors into time)
Summary: To prevent the selling of their ancestral home Martha and
Tad use the power of a magical ring to travel back in time.
    [1. Magic—Fiction.   2. Time travel—Fiction.   3. Dwellings—
Fiction.   4. Family life—Fiction.]   I. Title.   II. Series: McKean,
Thomas.   Doors into time.
PZ7.M478658Sf   1991   [Fic]—dc20   91-4447 AC
ISBN: 0-671-72997-7 (HC)   ISBN: 0-671-86690-7 (PBK)

Contents

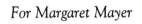

For Margaret Mayer

THE RING IN THE FIELD

It was Martha who found it.

It was a ring, and it fit the ring finger of her left hand perfectly.

The twins, Martha and Tad, and their brother, Joe, were in the field behind their house raking leaves.

"Rake them into one big pile," Joe had said in his bossiest big-brother voice.

"Listen, Joe," said Martha. "Just because you're older doesn't mean you're our father. Tad and I want to make our own pile. Don't we, Tad?"

Joe jumped in before Tad had a chance to say anything. "We always raked them into one pile before," he said. "And that's the way we're going to do it now!"

"That's what you think," said Martha, picking up a handful of leaves and tossing them at Joe.

Tad could see Joe was trying to control his temper. It was usually a lost cause.

Joe pushed Martha so hard that she tumbled to the

ground. At fourteen, Joe sometimes forgot how strong he was, especially when he was up against his eleven-year-old sister and brother.

Martha let out a howl.

"Oh, stop being such an actress," Joe said.

"I'm *not* acting," cried Martha, waving her left arm in the air. "I am wounded for life!"

"Good grief!" cried Tad, catching a good look at Martha's arm. "What did you fall on?"

"Oh, who cares . . ." Joe had begun, but by then they had all noticed the mark on Martha's arm. It was shaped like a circle. It was then that Martha found the ring.

"Take it off a minute, Martha," said Tad. "I want to look at it. It's almost the color of silver, but I'm sure it isn't. I don't think I've ever seen a metal quite like it. Maybe—"

"Maybe it was made in Hong Kong," said Joe.

"It must be an antique," Tad continued seriously.

Further examination uncovered two initials, T. F., etched on the inside and, on the outside, an elegant design of interlocking loops that were nearly rubbed smooth by time.

"It's beautiful," said Martha. Then, resuming her stage voice, she said, "I shall always wear it. Always."

"Tad! Martha! Joe!" came a voice across the fields. "Time to get ready for dinner."

It was the middle of October, and though it was still early, their mother had the lights on in the house. She stood in the kitchen door, silhouetted in the yellow light. Behind them, evening was settling over the fields.

"Mom," called Martha. "Look what I found!"

"It looks like it's very old," said their mother after inspecting the ring. "I'll bet it's been in the ground for a good long time."

"I knew it," said Tad. "Joe said it was made in Hong Kong."

"I was only kidding."

"Do you think it's as old as our house?" Martha asked.

"I don't really know; after all, this house is *very* old. It was built back in seventeen seventy-two—"

"And it's been in the Byram family ever since." Tad and Martha finished the sentence they'd heard at least two hundred times.

Bluebird Hall, the family's home, was an old, rambling Colonial house in the town of Rock Ridge, Massachusetts. It was filled with portraits and keepsakes of their father and his ancestors. Looking at these things sometimes made the children sad. It was only four years since their father had died after an automobile accident. The years hadn't been easy ones. Their mother had had a hard time making ends meet. Not too long ago, she'd even had to mortgage Bluebird Hall.

"More soup, anyone?" asked their mother when they were seated around the old table in the now somewhat shabby dining room.

"No? All right then, Joe, will you bring in the main course?"

A moment later, Joe appeared with a steaming dish and placed it on the table.

"Good grief!" said Tad, seeing what was in the casserole.

"Not again!" cried Martha, rolling her blue eyes. "I shall simply die if I have to eat liver one more time."

"Martha Byram," said their mother. "You know money is tight around here. And you know the butcher gives us a good price on liver."

"Probably because no one else will buy it," said Joe.

"Ugh!" said Martha, poking the meat on her plate with a fork. "I'm sick of things that are good for us. I wish we could have ice cream for our main course."

"Ice cream for our main course," said their mother in a strange voice. "Now *that* is a good idea. I wonder why I never thought of it before."

Like a woman in a dream, their mother left the dining room, humming happily to herself as she got ice cream out of the freezer and bowls out of the cupboard.

"Has she gone crazy?" said Joe.

"I hope not," said Martha.

"I don't get it," said Tad. "Unless she's so worried about having to mortgage Bluebird Hall that she—"

"Don't try to figure this one out, Computer Brain," said Joe. "I'd say we just entered the Twilight Zone."

"Why are you looking at me like that?" said Martha, noticing Tad's gaze. "All I did was wish we could have ice cream."

"That's it!" said Tad.

"What?"

Tad replied by tapping the ring finger of his left hand. Martha looked at her own finger—and the ring.

Martha's jaw dropped. Now she knew what Tad had figured out.

"It's magic," she said softly.

"What's magic?" said Joe.

"Nothing, Joe," said Tad as the dining room door opened and their mother appeared, carrying a tray with four bowls piled high with ice cream.

"All right!" said Joe.

Tad and Martha felt a bit nauseous eating a few bites of liver and then a heaping bowl of ice cream, but Joe and their mother didn't seem to mind at all.

"It *is* magic," said Tad quietly. "There can be no other explanation."

2

BLUEBIRD HALL

"Now we can *really* drive Joe nuts," said Martha, giving the ring a grateful pat.

Dinner was over and the dishes were cleaned up. Tad and Martha were in what the Byram family called the small attic. Because Bluebird Hall was so large, it actually had three different attics, each at a different level. Tad and Martha had chosen the smallest one as their private meeting room. After sweeping what had seemed like a century's worth of dust off the unfinished wood floor, they'd laid down an old braided rug, lugged up some chairs destined for the dump, and hung a few pictures on the wall. Tad had put up one of Albert Einstein; Martha, one of Sarah Bernhardt. They'd also put up one of them and their dad, taken the day they'd been brought home from the hospital.

Although Tad and Martha were twins, they looked very different. Tad was small for his age, with serious brown eyes and short, sandy-colored hair. Martha was tall and slim, her blue eyes always blazing dramatically and her long, chestnut-colored hair flying loose. Martha actually looked more like Joe than Tad. They both had the same blue eyes—"Byram eyes" they were called—and both were big for their age. But Tad and Martha were the closest friends. It had been that way since they were born—and was even more so since their father's death. For one thing, they'd needed one another, and for another, Joe had changed. He'd gone from being an ordinary older brother to being angry almost all of the time. "Give him time," their mother always said, but Joe kept on being angry, no matter what anyone did.

"What should we wish for first?" Tad asked Martha.

"I plan to wish for a unicorn."

"But they don't exist," argued Tad. "I don't think even a magic ring can produce something that doesn't exist. That would be wasting a wish."

"Who cares if we waste a few? We've got a ring full of wishes."

"Not necessarily," Tad said. "Haven't you read any books about magic? Magical things almost always come in threes. Maybe this ring only gives three wishes. Who knows?"

"What a lazy ring!"

"Ssh!" cautioned Tad. "Don't insult the ring! You have to be careful with magic."

"All right, then!" Martha said, interrupting. "I could wish for a new radio."

"Good grief," said Tad. "We haven't even thought about Mom or Bluebird Hall, or anything!"

"You mean all that stuff Mom was talking about yesterday—about how expensive it is to keep Bluebird

Hall running, and how she earns so little at her job?"

"Yes," said Tad, "and that she has so little money left in the bank, and that the property taxes are so high in this part of Massachusetts. And the worst thing of all, that Mom had to mortgage Bluebird Hall."

Martha looked a bit sheepish.

"Tad," she said, "I know mortgaging something is really serious. I just don't understand exactly what it means."

"It means that the bank gives you money. Then, you have to pay the money back, with interest. And if you're still broke and can't pay back the money, then—well— then you lose your house."

"Lose Bluebird Hall? But we've always lived here— since forever!"

"I know," said Tad. "That's why our wish should be something that helps Mom out."

"We could also wish Joe were a little bit nicer," said Martha, rubbing her arm.

"Don't worry, we'll get around to Joe later."

"How about if we wish I become a famous actress overnight and make piles of money? That would help Mom out."

At this moment the attic door crashed open with a bang. It was Joe. "What are you two up to?" he said. "You've been acting weird since dinner."

"No, we haven't," said Martha. "We've just been acting like ourselves."

"Yeah," teased Joe. "That's what I said. Anyway, I came up because Mom needs us to move some furniture in the living room so she can vacuum under the rug."

"Mothers sure pick the strangest times to start cleaning," muttered Martha as she and her brothers headed downstairs.

"Your sister seems to be oversleeping again," Mrs. Byram said the next morning. "She's just like her father, he loved sleeping late."

"We *did* stay up late last night," said Tad. "After we moved all the furniture, we ended up looking through those old photo albums."

"I think I'm looking more like Dad," Joe said, arranging his blond hair.

"So do I, dear," agreed Mrs. Byram gently. "Now, Tad," she continued, "please get Martha out of bed."

In Martha's room, Tad tried all the sister-waking techniques he knew—shaking, tickling, blasting the radio, even pretending he was about to read her diary. Nothing worked.

"C'mon, Martha," he said. "You can't pretend to be asleep forever. What's going on? Do you have a math test today?"

But Martha remained asleep, her eyes were shut and her breathing was deep and slow. She certainly looked asleep; there was something so still and peaceful about her. Martha usually overdid it when she was pretending. She would snore dramatically or open her eyes to peek once in a while.

Tad tried pinching her, but Martha didn't react at all.

"Mom," called Tad loudly. "Come up here, quick!"

Mrs. Byram soon appeared in the doorway of Martha's room, not looking terribly pleased.

"Mom," said Tad, "I don't think she's faking. I think something's wrong."

In a flash, Mrs. Byram was at Martha's bedside.

"Oh, my goodness!" she cried a moment later after she, too, had been unable to rouse Martha. "What could be the matter?"

Tad's logical mind clicked along, but even he couldn't come up with any malady that could cause someone to sleep this deeply.

"This is impossible," Mrs. Byram was crying, trying to shake Martha awake. "I know I heard Martha talking to herself when I got up an hour ago."

"She might have been talking in her sleep," suggested Ted. Then an awful thought occurred to him: Maybe Martha had wished to sleep this soundly so she could miss school for a day. What a dumb wish, Tad was thinking when his mother spoke.

"Maybe you're right. Her voice *did* sound somewhat dreamy."

"What exactly did she say?"

"Well, first I heard her yawn and say, 'I wish I could sleep forever'; and then, a moment later, I heard her say, 'I wish we'd never found the ring'—whatever that means."

"You wouldn't understand," Tad said, making himself look down at Martha's left hand.

The ring wasn't there.

Tad remembered that Martha had put it on the night before for their discussion; she'd thought wearing it might inspire her. Guiltily, he remembered that he'd meant to tell Martha not to wear the ring to bed in case she wished in her sleep, but he'd forgotten.

Mrs. Byram was trying again to shake Martha awake, still with no results. "I'd better call the doctor," she said.

Tad looked at his sleeping sister and shook his head sadly. "I don't see how a doctor can cure something that magic caused," he said. "And if the ring is gone, I can't even think of any way I can help you."

Less than an hour later, the Byrams' family doctor was at Martha's bedside.

Doctor Mayer was entirely mystified. "I've never seen anything like it," he was saying. "For now, I'm going to take some blood samples to send to the lab for analysis. Maybe that will give us something to go on."

Leaving his mother and Dr. Mayer with Martha, Tad wandered outside. Maybe, he thought, if Martha wished the ring had never been found, it went right back to where we discovered it. And that means it's back in the field.

Tad found the spot where Martha had fallen—and all their troubles had started—but the ring wasn't there. He returned to the house and searched all of Martha's secret hiding places just to be sure. No ring.

Soon Tad was sitting quietly in his father's old study, in his father's old armchair. He'd even put on his father's favorite old cardigan. It wasn't logical; but sometimes when Tad had a problem, just being surrounded by his father's presence helped him figure things out.

Tad knew no one would believe him about the ring.

11

What proof did he have? He'd just have to solve this by himself. But if he couldn't, would Martha sleep forever? The only hope was that the wish would wear off or the ring would reappear. But what if Martha had to go to the hospital? And what if their insurance didn't cover it? Tad spent a long time thinking about "what ifs" when suddenly a new "what if" came to him. What if there was some other kind of magic in the field?

As fast as his feet could carry him, Tad dashed back to the field and started digging in the same spot where they'd found the ring.

Dirt and small pebbles got under his fingernails, and a shard of glass cut him painfully; yet Tad persisted. It was a chilly morning, but sweat poured off him as he dug, stinging his eyes as it dripped down his face.

Then he found something. It was large and hard and smooth, but it wasn't a rock.

Tad scraped away more dirt until, lying on its side, still stuck in the soil, he could see a silver vase with a narrow neck and a thin, curved handle. It was elegant and old, and something told him it had been made by the same person who'd made the ring.

Tad lifted the vase and, at the base, only just visible to the eye, saw the same design of interlocking loops that had been on the ring.

Clutching the vase, Tad raced into the house and held his discovery gently to his heart. "I wish Martha were well again," he said.

Two seconds later, he heard his mother calling him from upstairs.

3

THE FIELD OF THE SEVEN WILLOWS

Tad raced up the stairs. In the upstairs hallway, he met his mother and Dr. Mayer.

"I'm sorry, dear," Mrs. Byram said, "but things aren't looking too promising. Martha didn't respond to any of Dr. Mayer's efforts to wake her."

"Are you sure?" Tad asked, not believing his wish hadn't been granted.

"I'm afraid so," his mother answered gently.

"One more thing," said Dr. Mayer as he prepared to leave. "I want you all to remain as quiet as possible so as not to disturb Martha. Also, on the chance that she is contagious, be cautious when you're around her."

"Doctor," Tad began, "what happens to people who stay asleep for a long time and can't wake up?"

Dr. Mayer considered for a moment. "That depends, Tad. In some cases, patients are put on life-support systems. But they can develop pneumonia and other maladies. I'd rather not dwell on that for the moment.

I'm sure we'll find an answer to this when I get the blood work done at the lab."

I wouldn't be so sure, Tad thought to himself as he showed Dr. Mayer out of Bluebird Hall.

Once the doctor had gone, Tad began examining the vase. Inside it but so far down it was unreadable, Tad found something engraved. The neck of the vase was too narrow for a flashlight beam to show whatever was written there, but Tad could make out that it began with two long words.

Growing up in an old house surrounded by antiques — and having had a father who had been, in fact, an historian — Tad hated the idea of sawing the vase in half. But he had to do it.

"Sorry, vase," Tad said a few minutes later as he placed it in a vise down in the basement of Bluebird Hall.

Scratch went the blade of the saw as it passed over the side of the vase. Then it snapped in two. Tad tried a bigger saw but soon had to give up. Whatever the vase was made of, the material was too strong to be cut by a handsaw.

"Mom," whispered Tad to his mother as she sat by Martha's bed. "I have to bike into town. Will you be okay?"

"Of course, dear. Joe's here, and I called your Great-aunt Ruth. She'll be phoning later in the day."

Twenty minutes later, and out of breath from bicycling so rapidly, Tad was in Rock Ridge's hardware store. It was run by his old friend Sam Wilcox.

"It goes against the grain," Sam said after Tad had explained what he wanted. "But if you say this vase has to be cut in half, well, I'll try 'er out on one of my power saws. But I sure would like to know why. I'd also like to know why you're not in school today."

"I'd tell you if I could," Tad said, "but I can't."

"Well," said Sam as he fastened the vase to the table of the power saw, "I've known you ever since you were a baby. And I knew your dad when he was a boy. I even knew your granddad. In fact, the Byrams and the Wilcoxes have been friends ever since Revolutionary War days, and I can't recall a Byram ever tellin' a lie about something important. So I'll do what you say, just as long as you're sure."

"It's the only way, short of an X-ray machine," Tad answered.

It wasn't easy, but at last the power saw made its way through the vase. Tad picked up the base of the vase, and with Sam's help, he was able to decipher the letters made from dots pricked into the metal.

TAMBURLAINE FIRSHADOW
FIELD OF THE SEVEN WILLOWS
1771

"My word," said Sam, "this here vase was over two hundred years old."

Although Sam knew nearly everything about Rock Ridge, he had never heard of the Field of the Seven Willows. "I'm sure it existed way back in the seventeen seventies," he said, "but it's probably gone by now, all built over and ruined and forgotten, like so many other things."

"But how could I find out where it used to be?" asked Tad. Maybe, he thought, just maybe, there might be something in that field that could help Martha.

"That shouldn't be too hard. Just head on down to the Town Hall and ask for the Historical Society's office. They've got all kinds of old maps and charts and whatnot, even goin' back to the seventeen seventies."

"Thanks, Sam," called Tad, heading outside for his bicycle. "Some day I'll tell you what this is all about."

Tad entered Town Hall just as Horatio Snivell was leaving. The Byrams and the Snivells were the oldest families in Rock Ridge; but while the Byrams had held on to their old home and the land around it, the Snivells had sold their house. It was razed, and the land around it had become a shopping mall. The Snivells had moved into a new split-level house. Before long, they had regretted their decision and had been trying to get their hands on Bluebird Hall ever since. Although Mr. Snivell was the tax commissioner of Rock Ridge, Mrs. Byram always said he was the most dishonest man in town.

Mr. Snivell eyed Tad with his beady eyes but said nothing as they passed.

"I wouldn't talk to him if he were the last man on Earth," said Tad to himself, which was exactly what Tad's father had always said about Mr. Snivell.

"Before I answer your questions, young man," began

the prim, silver-haired woman who ran the Historical Society's office, "I should like to know why you are not in school."

Tad disliked lying, but he felt there wasn't a second to lose—waiting until after three o'clock might be too late.

"This is my study hall period," he said quickly, "and they let me leave school so I could do research for a school report on . . . on our town back in the seventeen seventies."

"A most interesting topic," replied the woman, brightening considerably. "Now, let's see what old maps we can find."

It didn't take long to discover that the Field of the Seven Willows had been two hundred feet due west of where the river bisecting Rock Ridge made a sharp loop. The crinkly old map even showed who had lived there: Tamburlaine Firshadow.

Reaching the spot where the river looped, Tad stopped. It was hard to believe this was the same place shown on the map. Gone were the empty fields, the pastures, the little pond halfway between the river and the field. In their places were shopping centers, parking lots, and large, square concrete buildings.

Starting where the river looped, Tad measured off two hundred feet with an old tape measure, one of the many handy items he found in his pockets. He couldn't measure in a straight line—there were too many new office buildings—but at last Tad stood on what he thought was the site.

There weren't any willows, there wasn't even any

field. There was just an apartment building and a sign on a strip of concrete. SEVEN WILLOWS CONDOMINIUM it read, and there was a picture of a willow on the sign.

Tad sneaked into the building and combed all ten floors, but he found nothing unusual in the long corridors with rows of doors on either side. When the lobby attendant wasn't looking, Tad read every name on the mailboxes just in case a descendant of Tamburlaine Firshadow was living there. But there were no Firshadows.

Finally, Tad went down to the basement. A large heating system rumbled, and pipes wound along the ceiling. A few crates leaned against a cinder block wall.

Tad was heading for the far side of the basement, where he saw another room, when someone grabbed his shoulder. Wheeling around, he was confronted by a large, angry man he correctly guessed to be the building's superintendent.

"Get outta here before I call the cops!" the man said.

Never had Tad seen Martha lying this quietly. Her skin seemed especially pale, and her long, chestnut-colored hair, not neat at the best of times, covered the pillow on which she lay. The only sounds in the room, besides Martha's slow breathing, were Mrs. Byram's stifled sobs.

After escaping the super, Tad had bicycled back to Bluebird Hall, where he found the situation had gone from bad to worse. Calling from the lab, Dr. Mayer had reported nothing unusual in Martha's blood. The coma she had slipped into was not explainable scientifically.

"So what's next?" Tad asked his mother.

Wiping a tear from her eye, Mrs. Byram replied, "If there's no change in Martha's condition, she'll have to go to the hospital for observation and testing. Then, if there's still no change, they'll have to try some sort of therapy."

"What do you mean, 'some sort of therapy'?" asked Joe, who'd joined in the conversation.

Mrs. Byram looked even more upset. "Some kind of drug or perhaps electric shock."

"But that could be dangerous!" cried Tad. "What would happen if they gave her medicine for a disease she didn't have?"

"She's very sick already, dear," said Mrs. Byram, sighing. "If there's no change by tomorrow, we'll have to hire a nurse. Where we'll get the money to pay, heaven only knows. Then, if there's still no change, Martha will have to be transferred to the hospital."

"But they won't be able to help her there . . . " began Tad, then stopped. What was the point of talking about it when no one would ever believe him? Besides, a small but persistent voice in the back of his head kept saying, "You haven't finished exploring the basement of the Seven Willows Condominium. Go back there and finish the job."

The only problem was that Tad was scared to go back there alone.

"I-I've got something I've got to do," Tad said quietly.

"Now?" said Joe.

"Yes," Tad replied. "It's very important. And, Joe, I need you to help me do it."

Joe looked uncertain, but Mrs. Byram said to him,

"Go with Tad, Joe. I wouldn't mind some time alone."

Mrs. Byram remained by Martha's side, while Tad and Joe bicycled toward the center of Rock Ridge and the basement of the Seven Willows Condominium.

4

TAMBURLAINE

"I still don't see what we're doing here," grumbled Joe.

The two boys had successfully evaded the superintendent and were poking around the basement.

"I told you, I couldn't explain it," said Tad as he and Joe finished searching what had turned out to be an empty storage room—just four cinder block walls and a door that opened on to the rest of the basement.

"But I just had this hunch—" said Tad.

"Well, you were wrong," Joe said. Then, softening a little, he added, "Being upset can make anybody do some weird things."

There was nothing Tad could say as the brothers left the basement by a side entrance.

Outside, in the fading light of afternoon, they were about to get on their bicycles when Tad reached into his pocket and realized he must have dropped his house keys in the basement.

"I can't wait all day while you look," Joe told him. "I'm going back home. Mom might need us. See you later."

For the third time that day, Tad entered the basement of the Seven Willows Condominium. Something old that was unnoticed by anyone might be waiting near the earth, he told himself. That's what a voice deep inside him kept repeating: There could be something. There still could be *something*.

Tad found his keys in the empty storage room. A roughly lettered sign on the wall read: NO STORAGE HERE.

After putting his keys safely in his one buttoned pants pocket so they couldn't slip out again, Tad took a long look around the room.

What he saw took his breath away. He knew it had to be what he'd come to find. But it was impossible.

It was a door. But it wasn't just any door. And it hadn't been there a second ago.

Right in the middle of where the words NO STORAGE HERE had been printed, an old-fashioned wooden door had appeared. Intricate black metalwork curlicued across the gleaming wood. The doorknob looked like it was made of ivory.

Alone in the basement, Tad approached the door. A small metal plaque was at eye level. Engraved on it in an elegantly swooping old-fashioned script were two words: TAMBURLAINE FIRSHADOW.

Barely knowing what to do, Tad knocked.

Suddenly, the door opened.

5

THROUGH THE DOOR

The man who opened the door had on a ring that closely resembled Martha's, except that it was twice as wide. On his shoulder perched a white owl that examined Tad carefully with round, unblinking eyes. The man had an out-of-doors look, and his hair was black and shiny. Blue-green eyes looked down at Tad with keen interest.

"W-who are you?" said Tad.

"I am Tamburlaine Firshadow," the stranger replied. "Now step in. This door cannot remain open for long."

Tad found himself in what seemed to be a log cabin. The few windows were covered by roughly woven curtains, so it was impossible to see out. A comfortable sofa and a wooden rocking chair stood on a braided rug in front of a large stone fireplace with a fire burning in it.

"Find a seat by the fire," Tamburlaine said.

With his mouth hanging open, Tad collapsed onto the sofa. To steady himself, he leaned up against an orange cushion in the corner of the sofa.

The next instant, the cushion sprang to life. Uncurling before Tad's eyes, it leaped to the arm of the sofa, down to the floor, across the room, and out the window. Tad had just made out that the cushion actually had been a small fox when the stranger settled his lanky frame into the rocking chair.

"I found him when he was a very young cub," he explained. "He comes back once in a while to sit by the fire."

Tad didn't know what to say. All he could manage was to repeat his earlier question: "Who are you?"

"Just who I said—Tamburlaine Firshadow."

"But that's impossible," said Tad. "You can't be the same person who made the vase in seventeen seventy-one. You'd be over two hundred years old!"

"And so I am. Many things exist that one would imagine to be impossible. Let me show you another."

Rising from the rocking chair, Tamburlaine made his way to the window through which the fox had leaped and opened the curtains.

Tad looked through, and it seemed that his heart had stopped beating.

Tad knew he was in a basement in the middle of Rock Ridge. He knew that the view from this part of town—if basements even had views, that is—would be of the shopping centers, parking lots, and apartment buildings he'd passed on the way there. But Tamburlaine's window opened on to a field. Vines wound around a low stone wall, and a small vegetable garden was getting leggy with the coming of autumn. Far in the distance, beyond the field and a river, stood hills he recognized as the same ones he'd seen a million times before when he bicycled out of town. He knew the hills; but nothing else was familiar, especially not the field right below the window. There, Tad saw a grove of willows. He counted seven trees.

"Where am I?" he cried, suddenly frightened.

"There is no need for alarm," said Tamburlaine, resuming his seat, the owl still perched on his shoulder. "You are in a safe place. In fact, I have been waiting for you."

"But . . ."

"You see, I knew when you had found the ring, and later when you had found the vase. And I felt a deep pang when you destroyed it."

"I had to."

"I know all that," Tamburlaine continued. "You did nothing wrong. Actually, you were brave to come here and find me."

"Does that mean you can help Martha?"

"Not exactly. However, I can help you to help her."

Again Tad noticed Tamburlaine's ring. "Can you lend me your ring so I can wish Martha awake again?"

Tamburlaine shook his head. "I am afraid not. Some other time I will tell you more. For now I can only say that my ring, although much stronger than the one Martha wished away, gave but one wish. That wish was granted long ago when this country—and I—were still young although the land was already old. Once there were four rings. Two of these rings were joined together to make the one I wear. The third I buried in the field behind Bluebird Hall—"

"That's where I live."

"I know. I have been there. Now, there was a fourth ring, stolen a long time ago. Although lost in the present, that ring can be found in the past—if you are willing to look, that is."

"I'd do anything," said Tad.

"I know. Still, although I can send you through a door in time to where the ring is, once you are there, I will not be able to help you. You will have to search by yourself. And it could be dangerous."

"I don't think I really have a choice," said Tad.

"No," Tamburlaine agreed. "I would say that you did not."

"Could I go home and tell Mom I have to go somewhere?"

"I am afraid not. The border between my world and yours is constantly shifting. I cannot always guarantee it will be there when needed. And I can tell you, there is no time to lose. Martha must on no account go into the hospital and be treated for what is not a disease, as we both know, but is a result of magic and magic alone."

"Well, could I just phone Mom? Do you have a telephone?"

Tamburlaine laughed. "What do you think?"

"I think I'd better get ready to find the ring," Tad replied.

Laying a hand on Tad's shoulder, Tamburlaine pointed to the wooden wall directly behind him. Slowly, the very grain of the wood seemed to turn into currents of water. Tad could see the form of a door appear before his eyes. It took only seconds; but when the grain of the wood stopped moving, the door was complete.

Half in a dream, Tad let himself be escorted to the door by Tamburlaine.

"Go in peace," Tamburlaine told him. "Return in peace."

Tad opened the door and stepped through.

6
TRAITORS

Stepping through the door, Tad found himself in a forest. Sunlight sparkled on the leaves, and birds called from the trees. The doorway—and Tamburlaine—had vanished. As far as the eye could see, the forest stretched out around him.

Taking his position from the sun, Tad decided to walk west. He had no idea where he was, or even *when* he was; but he figured he should keep walking in one direction in the hope that he'd get somewhere sooner or later. Tamburlaine wouldn't have sent him to the middle of nowhere—or would he?

Tad's thoughts were interrupted by the sound of footsteps. Quickly, he hid behind an evergreen just as a man entered the clearing where Tad had been standing.

Once he got used to the man's long waistcoat, tight breeches, and funny shoes with buckles, Tad decided the stranger seemed to be trustworthy. He was about to step forward and introduce himself when a second man arrived in the clearing.

The two men shook hands, then looked around nervously.

"Did anyone follow you?" asked the first man.

"I think not," the second replied, "yet spies are everywhere. One cannot be too careful."

"Well said. I myself had the thought I heard footsteps nearby, but perhaps my ears deceived me."

"What is the plan?"

"The meeting is set for this very night," came the answer, "in the back room at the Town Hall."

"The Town Hall? Is that not too public?"

"Not at midnight. Nor will they expect us to choose such a location. In vain may they put guards about our houses. We shall not be at home!"

"Who is to attend?"

"All who may. Spread the word, but only to those about whom we may be sure. One word to the wrong man and we should all be shot as traitors."

The two men again shook hands. Then they parted company, leaving Tad deep in thought.

Suddenly, Tad felt a heavy hand on either shoulder and found himself looking up at a third man. Tad's eyes widened in astonishment. The man looked remarkably familiar.

"Who are you?" Tad cried.

"It is I who shall ask the questions," the man replied brusquely. "And the first is, What are you doing here?"

"Uhh—I'm not sure yet."

"What do you mean, you are not sure?" the man demanded.

Tad tried to think of a reasonable answer. "I'm—I'm on a bird walk, like John J. Audubon."

The man examined Tad suspiciously. "This man Audubon is unknown to me. Doubtless he is a traitor— like yourself!"

The man tightened his grip on Tad's shoulders.

"I'm no traitor!" cried Tad.

"I am glad to hear it,"the man answered. "For if I were to find that you were, you would pay with your life, even though you are but a lad."

Shivering a little, Tad looked closely at the man's face. Why were those beady eyes, that pointed nose, that receding chin so familiar? Then the answer came.

"Am I in Rock Ridge?" Tad asked first.

"Of course," replied the stranger.

"Then, is your name Snivell?"

The man squeezed Tad's shoulders so hard they hurt. "How do you know that?" he demanded. "You must be a spy—and a traitor! I shall turn you over to the proper authorities."

Never in the two centuries that the Byrams and the Snivells lived in Rock Ridge had the two families been friendly. Yet, whether he liked them or not, Tad knew that the Snivells had always been upstanding members of the Rock Ridge community. There was even a statue in the town park commemorating their bravery during the Revolutionary War. According to Tad's mother, that was the last time the Snivells had been right about anything!

By now Tad had guessed that he must be back in the days of the Revolutionary War. The clothing the men were wearing was right for that period, and it made sense of all this talk about traitors.

Tad thought fast. He knew Mr. Snivell would never believe he had come from the future, even if they were both on the same side. Somehow, he had to convince him, and without really revealing from where he'd come.

"I know who you are because I was sent to find you," said Tad, "and to tell you something important. They showed me a photograph of you—"

"A what?" demanded Mr. Snivell, looking suspicious again.

Oops, thought Tad. I guess photographs haven't been invented yet. Aloud, he said, "I mean a drawing, so I'd know who you were when I saw you."

"Who did this?"

"I can't tell you their names, but they're on our side. And they have a very important message for you. It's about when the traitors will be meeting, and where."

"You know this?" asked Mr. Snivell.

"Yes, I do," replied Tad, and he told Mr. Snivell all he had overheard.

Mr. Snivell scratched his chin. "This is worse than we feared. The traitors are plotting against us."

Mr. Snivell nodded for Tad to accompany him, and the two set off through the woods. After a fifteen-minute walk, Tad noticed that the woods were starting to thin out. Soon he saw a house.

"Have we arrived in Rock Ridge?" Tad asked, as he thought, Good grief, so this is what it looked like.

"Need you ask?" said Mr. Snivell. "One would think you came from the moon, so strange do you speak and so strange, too, do you dress."

"Well," Tad replied, "at least I'm on the right side. And thank goodness you are, too."

Mr. Snivell shot Tad a peculiar look, tightened his grip on Tad's shoulders, and steered him toward the house Tad had spotted a few minutes earlier.

Tad could just recognize it. It was the Snivells' old house, the one they'd sold to developers. Tad recalled his father taking him, Martha, and Joe there shortly before it was to be torn down.

"This should be illegal," Tad's father had said, "and mark my words, one day the Snivells will regret it."

Tad's father had been right, but he'd died before the Snivells had tired of the split-level into which they'd moved. That was when they began trying to convince Mrs. Byram to sell Bluebird Hall, the oldest Colonial house left in Rock Ridge. But Mrs. Byram always said, "I don't care how broke we are, I wouldn't sell them yesterday's newspapers."

Ushering Tad into the kitchen, Mr. Snivell told him to take a seat at the table while he searched the larder for something to eat. Tad was thinking how odd it was to be sitting in a place that no longer existed when Mr. Snivell returned. Soon Tad and Mr. Snivell were wolfing down bread and cheese.

While he ate, Tad considered his next move. He had to find the ring. It must be back in Rock Ridge, in the 1770s—but where?

A knock on the door interrupted Tad's thoughts. A portly man darted in, face flushed, gasping for breath.

"I have news!" he shouted. "There is to be a meeting, but, alas, I do not know where!"

"We do! I overheard the traitors planning it. And I told Mr. Snivell everything, so they will be stopped."

"Thank the Lord!" the plump man exclaimed, taking a seat. "Now we can inform the governor; at least a few colonists are loyal to His Grace, the King."

"Loyal to the king!" gasped Tad. "But I'm not . . . I mean, I thought . . ."

"Then you thought wrong," sneered Mr. Snivell. "Help me with the lad!" he barked at the portly man.

In a flash, Tad was pinned between them.

"The young fool sides with the colonists!" pronounced Mr. Snivell.

While Tad struggled in vain, his two captors looked around them.

"The larder," said Mr. Snivell. "It has a good, thick door with a sturdy lock. He won't escape, try as he may. Later, we shall return and see what else he knows—after we have alerted those in charge to the rebels' plans!"

Before Tad knew what was happening, he was thrown like a sack of potatoes into the larder, and the door was bolted behind him.

Mr. Snivell snickered through the door. "Remember, lad, that at midnight, your friends, the traitors, shall meet the surprise of our guns. They shall be cornered and captured at the Town Hall—thanks to you! A British victory shall be assured. Yes, lad, your cause is doomed!"

In the cramped, dark larder, Tad sat slumped against a wall. Now there's no way I can get out of here to help Martha! he thought. And not only that, I've lost the war for the Americans. It's all my fault!

7

INTO THE NIGHT

There was no way out. Tad's shoulders soon ached from heaving himself against the door. He was trapped in the larder—and in the past. At that very moment, men could be dying because he hadn't had enough sense to keep his mouth shut.

Suddenly, Tad sprang to attention. Someone was in the house, moving around the kitchen.

"Drat!" said a voice. "I know my shawl must be about here somewhere. If I could but get one of these lanterns lit . . ."

It was a woman, not a soldier.

At once, Tad started pounding on the door of the larder and shouting at the top of his lungs. "Let me out! Help!"

To Tad's surprise, the woman began shouting, too.

"Lord save me," she cried. "It's an evil spirit!"

"No, it's not," Tad yelled. "I'm just a boy, and I got locked in the larder by mistake."

Very slowly, footsteps approached the larder door.

"Are you quite sure you are a child?" the woman asked.

"Yes," cried Tad. "I'm only eleven years old."

"Then why are you in my brother's larder?"

"I was just helping your brother out and got locked in here by mistake."

"Well," said Mr. Snivell's sister, "I am not sure I should, but you are but a child."

Next, Tad heard the wonderful sound of the door being unlocked and then opened. Stepping out, he saw a woman in her mid-fifties peering at him suspiciously. In one hand she held a lantern, and in the other a large envelope. It was startling how much she resembled her brother, even her squinty expression was the same.

"I never know what to expect in this house," she said.

"What do you mean?"

"I mean, my brother always seems to be up to something most unusual."

"You mean with the soldiers?" Tad asked.

"That," sniffed Mr. Snivell's sister, "is not unusual. It is our duty to assist the king as best we can. I suppose I should not be telling you this, but I am afraid my brother is delving into black magic!"

"Magic!" gasped Tad, suddenly thinking he must be in the right place after all.

"Yes, lad. I have seen him make objects disappear at his very command. In fact—"

But at this moment, the sound of hoofbeats galloping swiftly down the nearby lane interrupted the conversation. As they faded into the night, Mr. Snivell's sister quickly changed the subject. "Whatever am I doing," she said, "to be chatting away when I have such an important errand to be running. As soon as I find my shawl, I shall be off."

"Perhaps I could help you," offered Tad, curious to know more about this errand. "Perhaps I could run the errand for you."

"It is a chilly night," considered Mr. Snivell's sister, "and I am a bit weary. But no, my brother said I was to deliver this message myself into the hands of the British general at Woodbury, just ten miles from here."

"Set me free!" shrieked the woman ten seconds later. Tad had shoved Mr. Snivell's sister into the larder and bolted the door behind her.

"Sorry," he called, "but at least you won't go hungry in there. The larder's full of food!"

"You *are* an evil spirit," she shouted.

Picking up the lantern from where it had fallen, Tad set off to explore the house.

If Snivell is practicing magic, Tad thought as he made his way out of the kitchen, then he must have the ring. But he wasn't wearing it, so it must be hidden somewhere in the house. I'd better find it before he gets back. With the shrieks of Snivell's sister still echoing, Tad tried to imagine where someone like Mr. Snivell might hide the ring.

The stairs creaked and the lantern cast crazy shadows everywhere as Tad made his way to the second floor. Below, Mr. Snivell's sister had stopped shouting and was now concentrating on pounding against the door.

Tad finally found his way to a large room in the back of the house. In it were a four-poster, a wardrobe, and two bureaus. Setting the lamp down, Tad got to work.

As he started searching Mr. Snivell's bedroom, Tad remembered all the times he'd searched Joe's room. He and Joe had once had a game in which one would "borrow" something from the other, who would then have to find where it was hidden. But this kind of friendly competition had stopped when their dad had died. Overnight, Joe became more serious, and more angry. It was as though he thought he was suddenly too old to have fun. Still, Tad had become an expert room-searcher, and drawer after drawer in the bedroom revealed its secrets to his quick fingers.

From the back of the house, Tad could hear occasional sounds—and each time he got goose bumps. What if Mr. Snivell returned? What if Snivell trapped him here in the bedroom? What if he shot him?

It was terrible to consider, but with his practical mind, Tad couldn't help but wonder what would happen if he was killed in the past. Would his family ever know what had happened to him, or worse, would he suddenly appear back in the present, dead? He tried not to think about it as he went through drawer after drawer.

Mr. Snivell's bedroom revealed nothing of interest except that he had the world's largest collection of pipes.

"To the study, if there is one," whispered Tad to himself, setting off again to find his way around the dark house.

He was halfway down the stairs when he heard footsteps passing the house. Then they turned and came up the walk. Tad extinguished the lantern just as the front door opened.

Tad pressed himself against the wall and hoped the thumping of his heart wouldn't give him away. He peered down the stairs, which opened on to a small entryway leading to the front door. Tad could make out Mr. Snivell and his companion. Now they were accompanied by a third man.

"Yes," Mr. Snivell was saying in a low voice, "I sent my sister to Woodbury to alert the British there. I have alerted them here in Rock Ridge. There is no way the rebels can escape our clutches."

"Now we shall see exactly who is siding against the king, and they will pay with their lives!"

"But we must make haste," interrupted the portly man. "The general wished us to ride with all speed to Greenvale. With three troops of soldiers, we shall surround the traitors without fail."

"I look forward to seeing them squirm," said Mr. Snivell. "That is why I had to delay us ever so slightly. I wish to take my musket on this merry errand. When we left, I knew not that we should have the honor of fighting."

Just hurry up and go! Tad thought desperately, still trying to press himself against the wall. If one of the men so much as looked up the stairs . . .

"What is that?" cried the third man in a sharp voice.

They've seen me! thought Tad.

"I think I hear pounding."

"Oh, that," chuckled Mr. Snivell. "It is nothing but a young spy I caught this afternoon in the forest. He is a lad today but shall be a dead man on the morrow."

Tad swallowed hard in the darkness.

After Mr. Snivell removed his musket from a rack on the wall, he said, "One more minute, if I may. I have a little something in my desk that I believe might be more powerful against the rebels than any musket."

Good grief, thought Tad. The ring! If he starts using *that* against the revolutionaries, the war's already lost. In the darkness, Tad could almost see Martha asleep in her bed. And it's not only the war that'll be lost, he added sadly.

But the third man seemed pressed for time.

"I know of nothing more powerful than a musket," he was saying, "except a cannon. Let us make haste. We must get to Greenvale by eleven o'clock."

"But—" began Mr. Snivell.

"We cannot wait," interrupted the third man, who, if he were not more important than the other two, was at least more persuasive. "Let us go."

Tad heaved a sigh of relief as the three men disappeared into the night.

Once all sound of them had faded into silence, Tad relit the lantern. Fortunately, he had brought a book of matches with him. Pausing to adjust the lantern so it wouldn't burn too brightly, Tad smiled to himself as he thought of someone in the past finding a matchbook from the present. What would that person think, he wondered. It had the address of a restaurant in Rock Ridge on it that didn't exist in this time—not to mention the fact that matchbooks did not exist, either.

Entering Mr. Snivell's study, Tad had to laugh. "This is going to be too easy," he said out loud.

There in the study stood Mr. Snivell's desk—the same desk that was now in the Rock Ridge Historical Museum.

The desk had always fascinated Tad. He could remember his father showing it to him when he was very little. The curator of the museum had been a friend of Tad's father, and he had let them into the museum after visiting hours a few times.

Tad's father had shown him the secret of the desk.

"It's got hidden drawers," Tad recalled his father explaining. "You push a knob and that moves a panel. You slide the panel back and that reveals another set of knobs. You keep going, but only in a certain order, until you are able to open the secret drawer. Unless you know just how to do it, this desk is safer than a locked vault, and a lot less obvious."

Setting down the lantern, Tad concentrated, trying to remember his father's exact words. Tad could hear his father's voice drifting back from his childhood, almost as if his father were speaking from that very room.

As if listening to instructions, Tad set to work.

Pushed knobs revealed panels, panels revealed knobs, more panels slid. More knobs were pushed or pulled until, at last, a small panel at the side of the desk dropped down and the hidden drawer slid silently out.

And in the drawer was the ring.

8

THE CRY OF THE WHIPPOORWILL

"Where did you come from?" demanded a thin man holding a musket. "You seem to have stepped from nowhere."

"It's my sneakers," Tad started to explain. "They're great for moving around silently, but I guess they haven't been invented yet."

"You talk in riddles," the man replied, pointing the musket at Tad's heart.

Tad wondered how he could possibly explain from where he'd come. Just a few minutes ago, he had left Mr. Snivell's sister pounding away in the dark larder and had tried to find his way through the Rock Ridge of over two centuries ago. Even in the darkness, Tad occasionally had recognized familiar landmarks that still existed in the present. But soon he'd become completely lost. Even though he knew where the Snivells' property had been in relation to the Town Hall, little else remained the same.

Now that he had the ring, Tad had decided to warn the revolutionaries quickly before returning to save Martha. After all, it was his fault they were now in danger.

I hate to waste a wish, Tad had thought, but I *do* have to get to Town Hall before the British show up.

Making that wish, Tad immediately found himself being scrutinized by a circle of men, all carrying muskets, all in tight coats, and most with long ponytails. Tad stood surrounded on the second floor meetingroom of the Town Hall. No one looked especially glad to see him.

"Hey! I'm on your side—" Tad began to say when a man silenced him.

"You are unknown to us," he said. "Yet you know of our meeting tonight. We do not know how you even entered the Hall. Our guards are at all the doorways and saw no one pass. We can but presume you are a spy for the British."

"But—"

"Shoot him!" more than one man in the crowd was shouting.

"I'm not a spy! I'm an American!" said Tad. "And I've come to help you. I've got something really important to tell you. It's about the—"

"Silence, lad!" commanded one of the men. "We have greater tasks at hand than to listen to the prattle of a child. Tie up the boy," he directed two men at his left. "Lock him in the closet at the far end of the room."

"Not another closet," groaned Tad as a tall man approached, evidently the leader.

"No," he said, "let us not judge the lad a traitor before he is given the chance to speak."

"I'm telling you the truth," Tad burst out. "I wish you'd believe me!"

Suddenly, it was as though a bolt of lightning had shot through the men. For a moment, no one said a word. Then, in a softer voice, the man who'd ordered Tad shut in a closet spoke. "Perhaps I was too hasty. I know not why, but it strikes me that I have misjudged this lad. Since we are pledged to democracy, let us take a quick vote: All those who believe the lad, raise their hands."

Forty-seven hands shot into the air, and the forty-seven men surrounding Tad now looked on him with friendly expressions. In the candle-lit room, Tad heaved a sigh of relief.

"Now, then, lad," said the leader, "what is it you have to tell us?"

"The British are coming!" burst out Tad. "I mean, they know of your plans to meet here tonight. British soldiers from Rock Ridge, Greenvale, and Woodbury are converging to surround this building and capture the lot of you."

"How do you know this?" someone demanded.

"Mr. Snivell told me."

"That old traitor!" cried one man.

"Hang him!" shouted another.

"Silence!" commanded the leader. "Perhaps we shall have the opportunity to deal with the treacherous Snivell later. But now, we must leave before it is too late."

"And just run away?" one of the men cried.

"No, my friend," replied the leader. "They shall come to encircle us, or so they imagine. But we shall make an even larger circle—and encircle them. We can be sure," the leader continued, "that the British shall mass among the rows of spruce surrounding the Town Hall on all sides. When they have assembled, *we*, not they, shall commence the surprise attack. And this shall be our signal."

The leader gave a cry like a whippoorwill, but just different enough a cry so that no stray bird could set off the battle by mistake.

The men started filing out of the meetingroom. The single candle was extinguished. In the darkness, brightened only by pale moonlight, Tad watched the men disappear into the dangerous night.

Tad felt a strong hand on his shoulder. It was the leader. "Come with me, lad."

Guiding him gently yet firmly, the man led Tad sixty feet beyond the Town Hall. There they found a low stone wall through which the men had slid the barrels of their guns.

Tad lay next to the leader.

"I am Paul Wilcox," he said.

"Wilcox!" cried Ted. "I know some Wilcoxes—Sam, for one. He runs the hardware store."

"I do have one relative named Sam," John said, "but he is a farmer."

"I'm Tad Byram and—"

"Byram!" exclaimed Paul Wilcox. "Why, there are

Byrams aplenty in Rock Ridge; they live at Bluebird Hall."

"I know," Tad began. "I live—"

Stopping in mid-sentence, Tad felt the leader's strong stare.

"Aside from your clothing and your style of speech," the leader was saying, "you resemble any lad. Yet I know you are not just any lad."

"How . . ."

"I know this because I saw you arrive. One minute, there was but empty air; the next, you stood there." Fixing Tad with his piercing dark eyes, he asked, "Where do you come from?"

Tad paused and replied simply, "I come from the future."

"I thought as much," said Paul Wilcox. "How far have you journeyed?"

"Over two hundred years."

"And why did you come?"

"I guess I was sent to help you," Tad explained. "You see, what I came to get will help someone in my time, but could have done terrible things in your time, if it were left in the hands of the man who had it."

"I am not sure I understand," said the man, laying a rough hand on Tad's head, "though I know you speak the truth. But if you truly come from the future, perhaps you could answer me this one question. Do we win?"

"Win what?"

"Do we win the fight for the freedom of our land?"

"Oh, that—yes," Tad answered. "It takes a while, but

you win. And then America goes on to become one of the most important countries in all the world."

"Tell me not too much," said the leader, silencing Tad, "for I fear too much knowledge from afar. Yet," he continued, "I would know one thing more. After we win this war, are we then to be free from war?"

Tad's silence was answer enough.

Tad knew he should leave, but in a strange way, he had become fond of these men. He knew they were brave, and even though Tad hated war, he knew they were fighting for something in which they truly believed. In fact, they were fighting for Tad and all those who were to come after.

All was quiet as both Tad and Paul Wilcox lay in thought. But the quiet was short-lived. Almost invisible at first, dark shadows began moving along the road toward the Town Hall. They massed among the spruces surrounding the white square building.

Peering into the darkness, Tad could just make out that they were men wearing red coats.

Then things started happening all at once.

Putting his fingers to his lips, Paul Wilcox gave a loud call—almost like a whippoorwill. The men on all sides of Tad shifted position. Then the leader fired the first shot.

It seemed as though millions followed, small explosions reverberated all around Tad. As each gun fired, there was a small but intensely bright flash of light, temporarily blinding.

Shots from the revolutionaries rang out from all sides

of the Town Hall, and soon the British were firing back. Bullets ricocheted off the wall protecting Tad and his companions. Once again Tad wondered what would happen if he died in the past.

Pressing his small frame into the cold earth and praying no bullet would hit him, Tad could not help but look up occasionally to see what was going on around him.

To his right lay the leader, his face taut with concentration, firing and reloading and firing his long gun. Amid the bursts of gunfire, Tad heard an even more dreadful sound: that of men being wounded. Looking toward the spruce trees, Tad saw many a man fall.

Tad knew he had to go home.

As the leader was reloading his gun, Tad touched his arm as if to say, "I'm leaving."

Tad gave the ring a pat, closed his eyes, and said, "I wish I were back in the present."

A second later he opened his eyes—and saw the leader looking back at him with a troubled expression. In the midst of battle, Tad knew there was no time for conversation, so he tried wishing again. And again.

Nothing worked. Tad was trapped in the past.

9

IN TIME

"Listen," whispered Paul Wilcox in an urgent voice, "this battle is becoming too bloody for a lad. Can you not return to your own time when you wish?"

"That's the problem," said Tad as the leader let off a well-aimed shot. Either the ring was out of wishes, or it was just not working.

Once again reloading his musket, Paul spoke. "Two hundred yards behind us lies the home of my sister. If you stay pressed to the earth, move swiftly, and have the grace of God upon you, you may reach her house safely. Tell her I have sent you. She will take you in. But go quickly, before the battle worsens or turns against our side."

Paul ruffled Tad's hair and resumed shooting. So wild was the battle, he never looked back in Tad's direction.

It was hard work crawling rapidly but staying flat at the same time. It was especially scary doing it alone. Tad was soon drenched with his own sweat—the sweat of exertion and the sweat of fear. Stray bullets whistled by, and in the darkness, every shadow seemed to be a British soldier ready to shoot whatever moved.

Like a dream, or the light at the end of a tunnel, the house got closer and closer. Finally, Tad's fingers touched the wooden planks of the front steps. He could have cried with relief.

Too scared to stand up and use the brass knocker high above him, Tad raised his head slightly, and with one hand knocked on the door. No one answered. "Help!" he cried, but there was still no answer.

I can't be heard over the shooting, Tad realized. He knew he'd have to stand up.

As soon as Tad stood and began pounding with the knocker, a bullet hit him. At the same instant, the door opened and a woman pulled him in, out of the night.

Faint and with blood streaming down his cheek, Tad hardly knew what was happening. All he could hear was the whizzing sound the bullet had made before hitting him. Stumbling into the house, he felt hands holding him firmly and heard a woman's voice saying, "Who are you? Why have you come?"

With his last ounce of energy, Tad whispered, "Paul Wilcox."

Immediately, the woman's face became kinder. "Ah," she said, "then you are welcome. But you are wounded— come. Down in the cellar I can light a candle and not be seen. There I can attend to you."

Safe in the cellar and cozy in the candlelight, Tad looked at the woman's face. She had the same eyes and direct gaze as her brother.

"The bullet has but grazed the skin on your cheek,"

she reassured Tad. "An inch to the left and you would not be here. I shall put some alcohol on it. It shall cause you no harm."

After doing this, she fixed Tad in the same stare her brother had. "I can see you come from afar. And though I do not support any war, I turn none in need away. How may I help?"

"I don't know," gasped Tad. "You see, I'm not from here . . . I mean, I am, but I'm not from now . . ."

"I think you are overtired," said the woman.

"Yes, but that's not all. I have to get home to help my sister, but I can't!"

"You do not know where you live?"

"I know where I live, but I just can't get there. It's impossible, you see. No one could get there from here, except maybe Tamburlaine."

"Tamburlaine Firshadow?" asked the woman.

"You know him?"

"All know him. He is a wise man. He lives not far from here, in the Field of the Seven Willows."

"Can you take me there?"

"Yes," came the reply. "Once the shooting is over, I shall take you there. I can see you are a friend of Tamburlaine's. There is something in your look. Also, you wear the same ring as he. Now, I shall go upstairs for some drink. You may take this candle and look in the root cellar for food. It's behind that door."

As the woman left, Tad took the candle and walked to the low wooden door.

Oh, Tamburlaine, he said to himself, opening the door.

"Yes," a voice answered.

Holding his candle high, Tad stepped through the door. He no longer needed the candle. It was broad daylight, and he was standing not in a root cellar but in the living room of Tamburlaine's home in the Field of the Seven Willows.

"How did I . . ." began Tad.

"You called my name and I heard you," Tamburlaine replied.

"But am I in the past or the present?"

"You are in what you call the present."

"But why couldn't I get back before? I wished and wished, but it didn't work," cried Tad. "I thought I'd never get back."

Giving a half smile, Tamburlaine explained. "You see, Tad, the ring you have works only through space; it cannot work through time. You could only return from the past when the moment was right and your passage in time was meant to be."

"But what will Paul Wilcox's sister think when she comes back and finds I'm gone?"

Tamburlaine gave a broader smile. "I can remember her astonishment well. She came and saw me not long after. I explained as best I could. I think she believed me."

"And her brother," burst out Tad. "What happened to him?"

"That is for another time," said Tamburlaine. "But for now, you have no time to lose."

"Why? How long have I been gone?"

"Only a few minutes of your time, Tad, but enough.

Dr. Mayer wants to send Martha to the hospital."

"What?" cried Tad. "It'll take me at least twenty minutes to get from here back to Bluebird Hall."

"Fear not," Tamburlaine said simply, gesturing behind him.

As Tad watched, once again the wooden wall began to swirl before his eyes. Soon it had formed into a door—the door to Martha's bedroom.

Without even bidding Tamburlaine good-bye much less thanking him, Tad raced to the door, opened it, and was gone.

10

THE FOUR RINGS

"I'm afraid so," Doctor Mayer was saying. "I would like to transfer Martha to the hospital without delay."

"Forget it!" cried Tad, who had suddenly appeared.

"Tad!" said Mrs. Byram. "Where on earth did you come from? You just seemed to step out of thin air. And your cheek, it's bleeding."

"Never mind that," replied Tad, darting to Martha's bedside.

One hand on the ring, Tad bowed his head and said in a whisper, "I wish Martha would wake."

A sleepy yawn from the bed told Tad the wish had come true.

It was a confused Martha who looked around her.

"Thank heaven!" Mrs. Byram kept saying while Martha kept repeating, "What's going on?"

Soon Joe joined them, and Dr. Mayer pronounced Martha "fit as a fiddle."

"I've never seen anything like it," he said, shaking his head. "It's beyond explanation."

*   *   *

Only Martha learned the whole story of her awakening. Mrs. Byram and Joe were never quite sure what had happened. They tended to think it had been a medical miracle.

"I have *got* to meet him!" said Martha the night after her recovery. Of course, she was talking about Tamburlaine.

"You lucky devil," she said. "There I was asleep, and you were having all the fun."

"It wasn't all fun," Tad told Martha. Tad hadn't felt quite the same about his adventures after what he'd learned earlier that day from his friend, Sam, at the hardware store. Yes, Sam had said, he *had* had an ancestor named Paul Wilcox, and he had been a leader of the revolutionaries. However, he'd been killed at a battle at the Town Hall. The revolutionaries were the victors that night, but Paul Wilcox had paid with his life.

"No, it wasn't all fun," repeated Tad, but Martha didn't really believe him.

"This is it?" said Martha the following Saturday. Mrs. Byram was at last convinced that Martha was truly better, and she and Tad were permitted to go off together.

Their first stop was the condominium at the Field of the Seven Willows.

"I can't believe he would live in a condo," Martha said as the twins sneaked into the basement.

"He doesn't live in the condo," Tad explained. "It just

happens to be where he is, too. You'll see, if he's there."

Approaching the wall in the storage room, Tad was disappointed to see no door, just wall. As they were turning to leave, Martha gave a quick cry. Before their eyes, the wall was changing until the polished wood door gleamed in the dark.

Before they could knock, the door opened.

"I have been expecting you," said Tamburlaine. "Come in."

It was sunny in Rock Ridge; but through Tamburlaine's windows, they could see great sheets of rain plummeting down. Martha was speechless for the first time in her life. Tad was surprised at something else. Clear as sunlight, that's how he recalled the blue of Tamburlaine's eyes. But today his eyes were gray, the exact somber shade of the rainy sky.

"The earth needs both sunshine and rain," said Tamburlaine, acknowledging Tad's unspoken question.

Soon the kettle was boiling, and in front of a blazing fire, Tad, Martha, and Tamburlaine sat down for tea. The little fox joined them, contentedly letting Martha pet him.

"So," said Tamburlaine with a smile, "you are the girl who makes all the troublesome wishes."

Martha blushed, and the white owl, perched on Tamburlaine's shoulder, looked at her with a critical expression.

"Magic," Tamburlaine went on, "is never easy to control. It has a mind of its own. I have learned that, and like you, I have learned it the hard way. I am still learning."

"Can you tell us about your ring?" Tad asked.

"Yes, a bit," Tamburlaine replied as the twins settled back to listen. "Long, long ago, when I was only a boy, my father disappeared into the wilderness. We thought he had died, but one day he returned. He had been studying with a medicine man, learning all about magic. There used to be more of it, you know, back in other days. More people believed, and more people knew more about it. And much of what my father learned he taught to me."

Here Tamburlaine paused to pat a small silver vial attached to the string of beads he wore around his neck.

"My father's greatest secret was not how to use magic but how to create it. Almost anyone can find a ring and make a wish; but to make a ring itself, that requires deep knowledge. This knowledge my father possessed. And one day he used it, and I was there with him. Using ancient techniques, we created four rings—four magical rings. One, as you know, I buried, believing it would be found by the people by whom it wished to be found— you, as it turned out. The second was stolen. This is the ring Tad has rescued from the past. And, believe me, in whisking this ring over two hundred years through time, you have saved humankind from untold horrors. I dread to imagine the havoc Mr. Snivell could have created. Now, shortly before he died, my father taught me how to make the magic stronger and broader. After his death, I took two of the rings and joined them into one. This does not make the ring twice as strong. It changes the whole form of power. It would be like comparing a candle to the sun."

"But didn't you tell me your ring had given just one wish?" Tad asked.

"Yes, that is so. And in some ways, perhaps, it was a wish that went astray. But perhaps not. The day I joined the two together was one of unparalleled beauty. Looking around me, I wished that the Earth might always be as beautiful as it was that day."

"That sounds like a good wish," said Martha. "What do you mean, it went astray?"

"Just look around you," Tamburlaine replied. "I do not mean here, out of my windows. No, just look around Rock Ridge. Can you truly say it is as beautiful now as it was then?"

"Good grief, no!" exclaimed Tad, "and I should know. But then what happened to your wish?"

"Somehow my wish created a whole other world—a shadow land, a world existing alongside your world. In this separate world, each tree, each leaf, each fern grows as it was meant to. And I, it seems, was included in this wish and am now the caretaker of this world. The world you see out my window is the world that was and, I suppose, the world that could yet be."

"But what good is it?" demanded Martha.

Tamburlaine paused to sip his tea. "That is a question I have often asked myself, for this is not the way I would have chosen for my wish to be granted. As I have told you, magic has a mind of its own. You two are not the first visitors I have had here, nor are you the only."

"You mean other people from our time get to come here, too?" asked Tad.

"Yes, and not only from your time but from the future,

too, and the past. And other times, too—times I could not explain. I cannot say what they bring back with them when they leave here. I can only hope they will wish to make your world less the way it is and more the way it could be."

"I've got another question," said Tad. "Why are those Snivells always out to get their hands on Bluebird Hall?"

"That is a good question. To put it simply, Bluebird Hall is a special place—an important place. And, I am afraid to say, the Snivells are a dark, shadowy bunch. Sometimes evil is attracted to good. Bad wishes to possess good, and ultimately to destroy it."

Tad and Martha remained silent and thoughtful even after Tamburlaine had finished speaking.

Gazing at Tamburlaine, Tad saw his eyes were again blue. Outside, he saw the rain had stopped.

"Let us take a walk," Tamburlaine suggested.

Soon the three were strolling through field and forest, shaking raindrops off low branches and picking autumn flowers. As they walked, Tamburlaine explained that Tad's ring, like Martha's, gave but three wishes a month. This, said Tamburlaine, was because the rings contained limited amounts of magic, and like any living thing, magic needed time to recover. To wish Martha's ring back, they would have to wait until the first of November, when Tad's ring would again be usable. Tamburlaine suggested that when the vanished ring was restored, one of them should be returned to him. One ring, he said, might be quite enough for the two of them.

Tad and Martha agreed.

"Where did my ring go?" asked Martha as the three watched a great blue heron take off ten feet to their left.

"You sent it to no space," replied Tamburlaine, "where it will remain until you call it back. No one else can get to it there but you and I."

While Martha climbed a tree to get a better view of the hills beyond, Tamburlaine told Tad to walk to a small pond near the grove of willows.

"There is someone waiting who wants to see you," said Tamburlaine.

Slowly, Tad approached the pond. The willows' reflection in the green water seemed very peaceful and somehow soothing. Tad saw a man leaning against a willow. In the willow's shade, Tad couldn't make out who it was at first. Then he could.

It was Paul Wilcox, looking well and happy.

"I'm sorry—" began Tad, but the man quieted him with a gesture.

"There is nothing to be sorry about," he said. "I am where I wish to be. And I was glad to learn you had made it back safely to your own time."

"Who was that by the pond?" Martha wanted to know.

"I'll tell you about it later," Tad answered as the twins rejoined Tamburlaine and hiked back to his cabin.

At the door to the basement, Tamburlaine gave brother and sister a big hug.

"Until the first of November," he called as they stepped back into the basement.

"Good-bye!" they called as the door vanished.

* * *

At school the following Monday, Tad's first adventure into the past had its last chapter. He and Martha were at an assembly. The subject was the American Revolution, and the speaker was Mr. Snivell.

"Yes," Mr. Snivell was boasting, "my family did its part and more in our battle for independence. We risked life and limb fighting the British! No family did more than ours."

On and on he went, perhaps believing his lies, until Tad could not contain himself any longer. Bursting into uncontrollable laughter, Tad was soon joined by Martha; and the two were quickly escorted from the assembly by the school principal.

"How could you be so rude?" she said. "I will have you know that all of Mr. Snivell's ancestors were fine, upstanding patriots."

"All of Mr. Snivell's ancestors were fine, upstanding traitors!" said Tad.

11

THE TREASURE

"What rotten luck!" said Mrs. Byram. She was sitting at her desk in the study of Bluebird Hall, sorting through her bills. It was an activity guaranteed to put her in a foul temper.

"What's rotten luck?" asked Tad from the sofa where he and Martha were playing cards.

"To be broke and to owe money when the tax commissioner is Mr. Snivell."

"But he can't just raise our taxes because he wants Bluebird Hall," said Martha. "Can he?"

"Not exactly. But what he can do is appraise our property at a higher value so we have to pay more property tax. And that's just what he's done, the worm."

"But can't we complain or something?" asked Tad.

"Yes," replied Mrs. Byram. "I requested what's called a reassessment. The committee not only approved the higher tax, they doubled it! Mr. Snivell is a powerful man in Rock Ridge. I'm sure he told them to make me pay more, or else. I can't prove my suspicions. It would be my word against Mr. Snivell's, and he'd win."

"But that's not fair!" cried Martha.

"I know, dear," said Mrs. Byram, sighing. "Life's often not fair. If I can't keep up with the payments on the mortgage, Bluebird Hall will be taken over by the bank—and soon by Mr. Snivell. I feel I fell into a trap set by him. He knows everybody at the bank. Well, I've asked for a raise at work, and that should cover things."

Tad looked at the calendar above his mother's desk. "Maybe something will come along soon to change our money situation around."

"We'd have to strike oil," Mrs. Byram said, smiling, as she returned to her calculations.

"What's up?" demanded Martha later that night as she and Tad met in the small attic. "I need my beauty rest."

"You've rested enough recently to last a lifetime," said Tad. "Listen, it's almost Halloween."

"So? I've already picked the costume I'm wearing to the party at—"

"That's not what I'm talking about. I'm talking about the day *after* Halloween."

"The day after Halloween . . ." Martha trailed off. "I don't get it."

"November first," prompted Tad.

"So?"

"We get your ring back, and we get to make more wishes."

"Of course," said Martha. "How could I forget?"

"Well," said Tad, "first we use my ring to wish yours back, then we return mine to Tamburlaine. Then we can start using your three wishes to change our money situation."

"Are we going to wish we'll strike oil in the backyard the way Mom suggested?"

"No," said Tad. "We won't strike oil, we'll just strike it rich!"

At Tamburlaine's, Martha's ring was soon wished back and the one Tad found returned.

"Can we have it back if we ever need it?" asked Martha.

"I am afraid not," said Tamburlaine, shaking his head. "Once you relinquish a ring, it passes out of your keeping; and like a shooting star, it rarely passes the same spot twice. Do you still wish to give it up? If not, it is yours to keep."

Tad looked at Martha and Martha at Tad.

"Something tells me," Tad said, "that one ring is all we can handle. All right, Martha?"

Martha nodded agreement, and Tamburlaine smiled and put the ring in his pocket.

The twins then told him about the danger facing Bluebird Hall.

"We've just got to find a way to wish Mom out of debt," Tad said.

"You had best think it over very carefully," Tamburlaine cautioned. "Wishing can be tricky. And besides, perhaps there is another way."

Saying that, Tamburlaine became silent.

"What is it?" said the twins, speaking at once.

"Just a thought. Perhaps wishing for wealth is useless when wealth might already be yours. I recall it being said that there was a treasure somewhere at Bluebird Hall. I know not what, nor do I know where."

"A treasure." Martha whistled. "Wow."

"Do you recall ever hearing about such a thing?" Tamburlaine asked the two, but neither had. "Then," he continued, "what I would suggest is that you speak with some older relatives. They often recall events others never knew of or have forgotten."

"We don't have many relatives," said Tad. "Aside from our Great-aunt Ruth, all we have is a distant cousin named Edith, and she's our age, anyway."

"Then why not begin with your Great-aunt Ruth," Tamburlaine suggested. "It is often best to get what you want by yourselves and leave magic out of it, *if* you can."

"I guess so," said Martha, a bit disappointed.

"Another thing," said Tamburlaine later as the three were sitting outside, roasting corn and potatoes over a small campfire. "Isn't there someone else in your family who might profit by coming here?"

"Mom?"

"She might," considered Tamburlaine. "But, oddly enough, few and far between are the adults who find their way here. No, I was thinking of someone else."

Tad thought for a moment. The leaves were at the end of their autumn colors and most had fallen, so the curve of the hills could be seen. It was a crisp November afternoon, not a cloud was in the sky; and aside from the crackling of the fire, a peaceful silence spread out around them.

"I suppose you mean Joe," Tad said finally.

"I suppose I do," said Tamburlaine. "He is your brother."

"But he's so —" began Martha.

"I know," interrupted Tamburlaine gently. "But remember, you two have each other. And remember, too, that he is the eldest; and when your father died, that could have been hard, as well."

Tad nodded. "You're right. Joe must have felt especially alone when Dad died, and I think he felt he had to take his place."

"Don't you think coming here would do Joe some good?" asked Tamburlaine.

"But when I brought him to the basement, the door didn't appear until he left."

"I know, Tad," Tamburlaine replied. "That *is* a problem. Before you can bring Joe here, you will have to get him to believe that there is a here to come to."

"We're going to have to be really careful with our wishes," said Tad as they headed for home.

"We could just wish to find the treasure Tamburlaine talked about," Martha suggested.

"But what if there isn't any? Then we've wasted a wish."

"We'd still have two left."

"The way *you* wish," teased Tad, "we need two in reserve to undo the first one!"

Reluctantly, Martha took off the ring and gave it to

Tad. "Why don't you wear it?" she said. "Who knows what I'm liable to say." Martha considered for a moment. "We could just wish Mom would get her finances all settled, and then we'd each get a wish, too!"

"I think we're forgetting something," said Tad. "Or should I say someone."

"Who?"

"Joe. I think Tamburlaine really wants us to bring Joe to see him."

Martha brushed a strand of hair behind her ear. "Well, even Tamburlaine isn't right all of the time. And, anyway, you did try."

"I know, but maybe I didn't try hard enough. Maybe we should wish Joe would believe in—"

"Tad," interrupted Martha. "I should have told you this before, but do you know that book of yours you love so much—that old science book Dad gave you for Christmas a long time ago?"

"Of course I do."

"Well, Joe borrowed it last week, and he spilled hot chocolate all over it."

"But that book was given to me by Dad. And Grandad used it when he was a boy."

"Joe knows that," said Martha.

"But how could he borrow it without asking and then be dumb enough to drink cocoa while he was reading it?" demanded Tad.

"Well," said Martha, "Joe is kind of a pig."

"Kind of a pig? I wish he *were* a pig. Then I'd sell him to a farm!"

"Listen, Tad," said Martha, "after we get Mom's

money troubles straightened out, I'll give you one of my wishes so you can wish your book was unruined. Okay?"

"Thanks, pal," said Tad. "You're the best twin a twin ever had."

"Shoo, shoo! Get away from me!"

Back at Bluebird Hall, Tad and Martha stopped outside the front door, where even the deer-head brass door knocker seemed to be listening to the shouts coming from inside.

"That's Mom!" cried Martha. "What's going on?"

"Let's hurry up and find out," said Tad, pushing open the door.

Racing into the house, Tad and Martha found an amazing sight. Their mother stood in the living room, cornered by an enormous pig.

"Shoo, shoo!" Mrs. Byram kept shouting while the pig was squealing, "*Oink, oink!*"

"Tad, Martha," she cried, catching sight of them. "Help!"

There followed the Great Chase. Tad went to fetch a long rope, while Martha began pummeling the pig with a big pillow. When Tad returned and the pig saw the rope, it made a mad dash for freedom.

Up the front stairs it charged, with Tad, Martha, and Mrs. Byram in pursuit. Along the upstairs hallway it thundered, its trotters making a racket on the wood floor. Then down the back stairs it plummeted. It missed the two steps where the narrow staircase turned and rolled squealing into the kitchen, where it momentarily lay stunned.

A moment was all Tad needed. Before the pig could find its feet, Tad tied it up tightly.

"But where could it have come from?" asked Mrs. Byram. "There isn't a pig farm for miles."

The pig, meanwhile, was struggling against its ropes. It looked right at Mrs. Byram, just as though it wanted to tell her something.

"You know, Mom," Martha said, laughing, "I think the pig likes you."

"I have to admit, it does seem that way," said Mrs. Byram. "But how it got into Bluebird Hall I shall never know. All the doors were shut. Perhaps someone is playing tricks on us. And on top of everything else, I haven't a clue where Joe's gone off to. One minute he was upstairs listening to the radio, and the next minute the pig shows up. I hollered for Joe, but he didn't answer. And while we were chasing the pig, I took a quick peek into his room. He wasn't there."

Martha noticed Tad had turned very pale.

He heaved a deep sigh, but all he said was, "Good grief."

Martha was still trying to figure out what was going on when Tad pointed to the ring.

Oh, no, thought Martha, shaking her head in astonishment. It had been on their way home. Tad had made a wish, though neither of them had realized it at the time.

It took some convincing, but Tad and Martha finally assured their mother that they'd take care of the pig and that she could go and relax for a while.

Once their mother was out of sight, Tad said simply, "I wish Joe were himself again."

In a flash the pig was gone and Joe was there in its place—all tied up.

"What the . . ." Joe began as Tad and Martha struggled to untie him. "Why was I all tied up?" he demanded. "And why don't I remember anything about it except that I feel really weird."

Tad looked at Martha and Martha looked at Tad. Neither wanted to be the one to explain.

Finally, Tad began. "Listen, Joe," he said. "You may not believe this, but it has to do with something in the basement of that building we went to. You see—"

"Just drop it," interrupted Joe. "I feel as though I'd fallen down a flight of stairs. I don't want to hear any of your crazy stories!"

At dinner that night, Tad and Martha managed to convince their mother that the pig had leaped from a passing truck.

"Luckily, the driver was retracing his path," said Tad, "so I raced out and caught up with him. He took the pig back."

"What pig?" asked Joe.

"Hmmm," he said, after hearing the story. "I don't know why, but it reminds me of something—kind of like a dream you can't quite remember."

"Well, dear," said Mrs. Byram, "let's not worry ourselves. Let's just settle down to a good dinner."

Dinner that night was ham, and for some reason Joe

said he'd lost his taste for it completely. He even asked to be excused.

"Isn't that odd," said Mrs. Byram, "Joe's always loved ham."

"Thanks to you," said Martha as she and Tad were walking home from school the next afternoon, "we are down to one wish. So we'd better come up with a good one if we want to save Bluebird Hall."

"I know, I know. I'm sorry," said Tad. "But I have an idea. This time, let's write out a list of wishes and then choose the best one. That way we have less chance of messing up."

"Sounds good," said Martha, and then she started laughing.

"What's so funny?"

"I was just thinking how funny Joe looked as a pig."

"I know," Tad agreed, "but Joe didn't always act like a pig. Then when Dad died . . ."

"But that was hard on all of us," said Martha, "really hard. I still miss Dad every day."

"So do I," Tad admitted. "But it must have been harder on Joe. He's always trying to act like Dad, but he can't quite fill his shoes."

"I guess," said Martha, sighing. "But I'm still sorry we didn't take a photograph of Joe when he was a pig."

Tad and Martha laughed.

But there was no more laughter when they got home. As they came in the door, they heard the muffled sound of someone crying. It was their mother. She looked at the twins and said in a shaky voice, "I've been fired."

"What?" Tad and Martha cried, running to their mother's side.

"Fired," sniffled Mrs. Byram. "And Mr. Snivell's behind it, I just know it. You see, when I arrived home this afternoon, I received an anonymous phone call; and I'm convinced it was from Mr. Snivell. All the man said was, 'It's going to be a nice Thanksgiving—for some of us.'"

"But won't you get unemployment compensation?"

"Sooner or later, I suppose, but it won't be enough," said Mrs. Byram, tears rolling down her face. "Not with the mortgage overdue."

"When's the next payment?"

"November twenty-first," Mrs. Byram said, sighing. "If we don't have the money in three weeks, we lose Bluebird Hall!"

12

THE CLUE IN THE PICTURE

"I think we should have just gone ahead and made a wish so Mom could come up with the money," said Martha as she and Tad were rattling their way to Greenvale on a local bus.

"Tamburlaine said we should speak to Great-aunt Ruth first," Tad reminded her.

"I guess you're right," Martha said, sighing, as the bus slowed to a squeaky halt next to Greenvale's town square.

Great-aunt Ruth was their father's aunt, and, as far as they knew, their father's only close living relative. One reason Tad, Martha, and Joe enjoyed visiting their great-aunt was because they always got to hear about their father. Every time she came to Bluebird Hall, Great-aunt Ruth would pay a visit to the Byram family graveyard, which was tucked away in a little clearing in the woods. It was a small graveyard, the kind many New England families had in the past. In it lay not only their father but also Ruth's parents.

Looking at her now, it was difficult to believe that in her youth Great-aunt Ruth had been one of the first aviatrixes. She had flown all over the globe before settling down again in her tiny cottage in Greenvale. "I'd already had enough adventures to last a lifetime," she had said, "so I thought I'd try something new." What she'd tried was painting, and her detailed renderings of scenes from her childhood and her imagination had proved an unexpected success. Her other pleasures were her gardens and her small greenhouse. She'd never married. Tad and Martha could remember their father saying, "My Aunt Ruth is the most independent individual I've ever met."

"Come in, come in," she was soon saying to Tad and Martha. Blue eyes blazed out from an almost unwrinkled face. Her white hair was held back by two small barrettes. She had on the blue satin dressing gown she always wore around the house.

Looking around Great-aunt Ruth's small living room, Tad suddenly was struck by how similar it was to Tamburlaine's; both had the feeling of being a place of refuge. Tad wondered if the two had ever met.

Great-aunt Ruth considered their question about a treasure at Bluebird Hall for a minute before answering. "It's odd," she said, "but now that you mention it, I do recall my mother telling me long ago that indeed there was some sort of treasure hidden in Bluebird Hall. But no one had any idea what it was or, more to the point, where it was."

Great-aunt Ruth then peered curiously in the children's direction. "I rather fancy you two look different all of a sudden."

"Perhaps I've grown," suggested Tad, who very much wanted to be tall.

"It's only a bit over a month since I've seen you." Great-aunt Ruth smiled. "I would tend to doubt that you've grown much in that brief a spell. Nonetheless, you do look different. But, of course, you are twins."

"What has that got to do with anything?" asked Martha.

"I'm sure Tad would be at a loss to explain it scientifically, but you are, as you know, the third set of twins to live at Bluebird Hall. There were Jeffrey and Anne in the last century, and Timothy and Rosamond in the early part of this century."

"So?" said Tad. "Twins do run in certain families."

"That's not what I meant. No, it has been said that each set of twins was, well, let us say they were *different*."

Both Tad and Martha had a sneaking suspicion what "different" meant, but they both wanted to know more.

"No," Great-aunt Ruth said slowly, "this is not the moment for stories, but I can show you portraits of them. Martha, run up to my bedroom. In the top right bureau drawer you'll find a small leather carrying case. Please bring it down."

In the carrying case were a number of small frames. They were made of a piece of sturdy leather that folded, so the frames would open like a book. Each was tied shut with a sewn-on ribbon.

"These are not photographs," their great-aunt reminded them, "but hand-painted miniatures."

Very gently, Great-aunt Ruth reached out with her large hands and selected two frames. She did so not by sight but by feel.

"Yes," she said, "these two. Tell me, please, what it says on the small pieces of paper on the back of each."

"This one," said Tad, "says 'J and A,' and this one, 'T and R.'"

"Fine. Then we have the correct ones. Open them carefully and take a look."

The twins gasped at the same time. Although the portraits were tiny—no bigger than one and a half by two inches—they were extraordinarily clear and remarkably similar: Each showed two children, dressed in old-fashioned clothes, holding a book and looking rather serious. Then came the startling part. Behind the children, and with a hand on each of their shoulders, was someone they knew. It was Tamburlaine.

"I just located these recently," Great-aunt Ruth was saying, "when I was visiting a friend. Perhaps they'll provide some clue to finding your treasure. I remember thinking how odd it was that the same man should be standing behind both sets of twins, although the portraits were painted fifty years apart and by different artists."

Something in their great-aunt's tone made both Tad and Martha think she was hinting at more than she wished to reveal. Before either twin could ask any more questions, Great-aunt Ruth headed for the kitchen to get things ready for tea. Tad and Martha were left alone to examine the portraits.

"Maybe it's the setting," said Tad, digging for clues. "Both pictures are set in a little grove of birches. Maybe that's where the treasure is."

"Maybe it's Tamburlaine," said Martha. "He's in both pictures. Maybe he's the link."

"But he's—"

Tad never got to finish. A loud crash from the kitchen set both twins running to see what was the matter. They found Great-aunt Ruth standing amid a pile of broken cups and saucers.

"Oh, dear; oh, dear," she was saying, "How clumsy I've become. I managed to load up the tray with the tea things and then dropped it."

"You should have asked us to help," said Tad. He and Martha started cleaning up the mess.

"Right," agreed Martha. "You just go back in the living room, Great-aunt Ruth, and we'll clean up and bring *you* tea."

The twins had a lot to discuss on the ride home.

"I thought Tamburlaine knew more about our family than he was letting on," said Martha. "I'll bet those pictures do hold some sort of clue, if only we could figure out what it is. I think we should just go and ask Tamburlaine."

But Tad had something else on his mind. "I'm worried about Great-aunt Ruth," he told Martha. "I'm glad we listened to Mom and didn't tell Great-aunt Ruth about our money troubles. Did you notice that she had to find the pictures by feel? And it's not like her to drop things. I think there's something wrong."

"She's just getting old," said Martha. "After all, she is eighty-two. And she could see us well enough to think we've changed. You know, I'd say she was right; Tamburlaine would change anyone."

"I know," said Tad, "but that's the kind of change you *feel* more than you see, if you know what I mean."

"I do. And you're sounding less and less logical by the minute. The next thing you know, you'll be sounding like me!"

13

THE CHOICE

"Who is that outside in the bushes?" asked Mrs. Byram the following morning at breakfast. "I'm sure I saw someone next to the birch grove near the garage."

"Good grief!" cried Tad. "I wonder what he's doing here."

A moment later, Mr. Snivell found himself surrounded by Joe, Tad, and Martha. But if he was embarrassed to be discovered, he certainly didn't show it.

"You're trespassing," Joe announced angrily.

"For the moment, perhaps," sneered Mr. Snivell, "but only for the moment. Doubtless your dear mother has informed you that the bank is about to take Bluebird Hall. And when it does, Bluebird Hall will be mine. I was just thinking that this area by the garage would be the perfect location for a large parking lot."

"Just get off this property before we phone for the police," said Joe sharply, trying to sound as grown-up as possible.

"Fine," said Mr. Snivell. "But you know I'll be back.

Back to stay. There's no way your mother will be able to raise the money now."

"That's what you think, you old traitor!" burst out Tad.

That day, Tad and Martha spent the entire afternoon writing out a list of wishes. It wasn't easy trying to figure out a wish that would be foolproof.

"If we just wish to save Bluebird Hall," said Martha, "it could mean we're saving it for Mr. Snivell, not us."

"We could wish the bank would forget it had lent Mom the money," suggested Tad. "I wonder if that's dishonest?"

"How about this," said Martha. "We can wish to always live at Bluebird Hall. That way the ring can figure out for itself the best way to get us out of this predicament."

"That does sound good. But we should add that we get to live here as its owners. Otherwise, we could end up renting it from Mr. Snivell."

"Good point," said Martha, nodding. "I can see it all now," she began, "our home saved by our very wits, yet no one shall know . . . except you and me."

"Enough, Martha. I need more time to think."

"Fine with me. We can talk about it while we're cooking dinner. Remember, we told Mom we'd have it ready when she came back from visiting Great-aunt Ruth."

The salad was tossed and the casserole was warming in

the oven when Mrs. Byram's old station wagon rattled into the driveway at Bluebird Hall.

Though the dinner was good, Mrs. Byram didn't have much appetite. Just before dessert was served, she broke the news. "You know I spent the afternoon with your great-aunt," she began. "I always like to see her, but this time I also had another reason. I went to see if I could borrow some money. Ordinarily, I'd never ask Ruth, but I've been to every bank in the county. An unemployed widow with three children isn't the best candidate for a loan."

"Can Great-aunt Ruth help out?" asked Joe.

"She would if she possibly could, you know that. Ruth spent the better part of her childhood with your grandfather here at Bluebird Hall. I sometimes think she knows it better than I do. But no, she can't help us."

"But I always thought she had lots of money tucked away," said Tad, "money she earned from her painting."

"Not anymore, I'm afraid. You see, Ruth didn't tell us she's had some health problems lately. And it turned out that her insurance didn't cover much of the cost, which was astronomical. So she has very little left, barely enough to get by on, in fact."

"But will she be all right?" asked Martha.

Mrs. Byram paused. "Yes and no," she said finally. "You see, Ruth has some rare sort of cataracts. The doctors tried this and they tried that, but finally they concluded there was nothing that could be done."

"But what does that mean?" asked Tad.

"It means she'll lose her sight."

"Completely?" asked Joe.

"Yes," said Mrs. Byram. "And there's no way she'll be able to carry on alone at her age."

"But she could come live here with us," said Martha.

"I only hope there will be a *here* to come to," said Mrs. Byram in a sad voice.

"I've got it!" said Tad. "Great-aunt Ruth can sell her house. With the money she gets from the sale, we can pay off the bank, and then she can come live here with us at Bluebird Hall."

But Mrs. Byram shook her head. "No, dear. What Ruth prizes above all else is her independence. She must be allowed to hold on to that for as long as possible. Even though she loves us, she's always lived alone. I don't think it would be fair to ask her to change that now, before she absolutely has to."

"But her sight's already going," said Martha. "Tad and I noticed it when we visited her. What will she do when it goes entirely?"

"I don't know," Mrs. Bryam sighed. "But I do know what happens to a lot of older folks when they lose their independence. They just give up hope."

No one knew what to say. There had always been a Great-aunt Ruth to love, and there had always been a Bluebird Hall. And now both could be gone.

"Now what are we going to do?" wailed Martha after dinner that night when the twins had retired to the small attic. "We've got two problems, but only one wish."

Tad shook his head. "I love Bluebird Hall," he said. "It's our home, and it was Dad's home."

"But do we have a choice?" Martha wondered.

"I don't think so," said Tad, slowly putting on the ring.

14

BACK TO BEFORE

Mrs. Byram was so excited, she went to school the next day to tell Tad, Martha, and Joe the news. She found them in the cafeteria, gloomily eating their sandwiches.

"Mom," they cried, "what are you doing in school?"

"I had to let you know right away," she said. "I think our luck is starting to change."

"What's happened?" asked Joe.

"It's Great-aunt Ruth!" said Mrs. Byram. "She just phoned me. She went for a checkup this morning, and you'll never guess what happened. Both of her cataracts have simply vanished. The doctor's amazed; he's never seen anything like it. Isn't that wonderful?"

It *was* wonderful. Still, it was hard to be entirely happy when Mr. Snivell was about to take possession of Bluebird Hall.

"The money's due November twenty-first, right?" Tad

was saying. "And we're already out of wishes for November, right?"

"Right," agreed Martha. "So?"

"So we've got to find some way to raise the money Mom needs without wishing."

"What do you suggest? We're too young to get jobs, remember."

"I suggest we go see Tamburlaine, and fast!"

Tamburlaine shook his head slowly and gave Tad and Martha a thoughtful look.

"No," he said simply, "I cannot say what the treasure was supposed to have been, or if indeed there ever was one. You two have searched Bluebird Hall from top to bottom, yet you found nothing. Perhaps you should search again."

"Maybe we should," said Tad, "but in the past."

"Oh, please," pleaded Martha. "I never get to have fun anymore. Mom watches me like a hawk ever since the doctor said I shouldn't strain myself too much after my 'mysterious ailment'."

"Oh, Martha," said Tad. "Don't remind Tamburlaine about all that."

"As if I would forget," Tamburlaine said with a smile. He then became silent for a long time. Finally, he spoke. "Yes, I will send you into the past, though I doubt you shall find any treasure—at least not the one you are seeking. Indeed, you may find more than you expect. But there is a purpose to your going, a circle to complete. So if you are ready, the door awaits."

"Right now?" gasped Tad. "Couldn't we go home and pack?"

"If I know you, Tad, you already have more than enough in your knapsack to carry you through. Am I not correct?"

"Well, I do have my flashlight and some strong nylon twine and—"

"Just as I thought. But you must move swiftly. The door is there but cannot stay long."

Looking behind Tamburlaine, the twins saw a door shimmering on the far side of the room. Holding hands, they approached it.

"Does it hurt?" asked Martha as they drew close to the door.

"Does what hurt?"

"Time travel."

"No, it doesn't hurt. But it does feel awfully funny."

And that was exactly how it felt. After Tamburlaine had opened the door and ushered them through, there was one shining moment when they were surrounded by bright light. Then came the sensation of falling rapidly, plummeting through layers of light and darkness. All this lasted less than a split-second. When it was done, they felt themselves alighting on ground again, yet with the strange feeling of never really having left it.

Still holding hands, they looked around expectantly. Both were disappointed.

"What a mean trick!" complained Martha. "All this talk about time travel, and we end up right back in our own kitchen."

"No, wait a minute," said Tad. "This is our kitchen, but it isn't!"

It *was* their kitchen, but not exactly. All the doors and windows were in their familiar places. The walls were the same color, and the same kitchen table on which they ate breakfast every morning was in the same place in the corner. But it wasn't really *their* kitchen.

Gone were the refrigerator and dishwasher, the electric light fixtures, even the stove. Instead there were oil lamps on the walls. The fireplace they now used for fun was used for cooking. A large brick oven was built against one of the outside walls.

It was a sunny day in spring, so warm that they soon took off the sweaters they'd been wearing when they'd left the present on a chilly November afternoon.

"You know," said Martha, "I think I like the way it looked then better than the way it looks now."

"I think I do, too," agreed Tad. "I wonder what year we've come back to? Well, I guess we'll find out pretty soon."

Tad and Martha were just about to explore the rest of the house when they stopped in their tracks.

"Did you hear what I just heard?" asked Martha.

"Yes," answered Tad, shivering.

"What was it?"

The two listened, and again they heard it.

From somewhere beyond the kitchen, out among the budding trees and the tender new grass, there came a horrible, unearthly moan. It produced its own echo, just as frightful as the original sound.

Tad and Martha ran to the window and looked out through the hand-blown glass.

"There's no one out there," said Tad.

"It's a ghost," Martha told him through clenched teeth.

"There're no such things as ghosts," whispered Tad.

"There's no such thing as time travel, either," shot back Martha. "I knew we should have stayed home."

"But you were the one who wanted to come."

"Well, I changed my mind."

Another heart-stopping moan echoed across the yard.

"It seems to be coming from underground," Tad announced.

"Then it's a dead person," said Martha. "How totally gruesome!"

"Perhaps it's the treasure, calling to us," said Tad.

"If it was the treasure wanting to be found, it would make a nice noise," Martha countered.

"I say we go look."

"I say you're crazy, but you're probably right. Let's go."

Bright sunlight warmed their faces as the two stepped through the kitchen door into the backyard. The large meadow behind Bluebird Hall had once been a garden, and many of the larger trees they knew so well didn't exist at all in whatever time they had come back to.

It would have been a lovely stroll if it weren't for the moans that stopped and started, started and stopped. Yet looking across the lawn and field and behind the garden walls, neither Tad nor Martha could see anyone.

"I told you it was a ghost," Martha was saying when

the cries sounded again. "I think they're coming from over there," she continued, pointing to a stone circle about eighteen inches tall and five feet in diameter.

"But no one could be hiding behind something that low," argued Tad. "It's impossible."

"Just about everything that's happened to us lately has been impossible," said Martha, running over to examine the low circle of stones.

Tad soon joined her, and they saw the beginning of a wall around a newly dug well. The twins could see no water as they looked down into it. They could, however, make out a dark form at the bottom. But whether it was a person or an animal, alive or dead, they couldn't tell—until it started groaning.

Tad quickly took the flashlight from his knapsack and shone it down the well. It had a strong light and could illuminate even the bottom of the thirty-foot-deep well. What it showed, hunched at the bottom and looking hurt and miserable, was an old woman.

"It looks like Great-aunt Ruth!" burst out Martha, squinting into the well.

"No, I don't think so. Whoever's down there looks skinnier than Great-aunt Ruth."

"Hello down there!" cried the twins. "Are you all right?"

The old woman peered up but was momentarily blinded by the glare of Tad's flashlight. He shut it off, and at last the woman spoke. "I think so," she said softly. "I must have fallen in. However shall I get out? And who are you?"

"One question at a time," Tad shouted down the shaft. "First we get you out."

Tad wasted no time in removing the nylon twine from his knapsack. He sent Martha to retrieve their sweaters. He knotted these into a seat and attached two long pieces of twine that he and Martha had knotted at twelve-inch intervals—"For easier handling," Tad had explained.

"Sit on the sweater part," Tad called down into the well, "and hold on tight. We're going to pull you up."

The sweaters and the twine were lowered into the well. Soon the old woman had positioned herself on the sweater-seat and was clutching the twine in either hand.

"I believe I am ready," she cried in an uncertain voice.

"Let's hope she's strong enough to keep holding on," whispered Tad. "She seems to have fallen in once without harm. The second time she might not be as lucky."

Tad and Martha then tied a piece of twine around their waists. Side by side they started walking away from the well. It hurt their waists, but Tad was convinced it was safer than simply trying to haul her up by pulling the twine with their hands.

Step by step, foot by foot, they struggled. Then Martha's twine gave a horrible lurch and went slack. For a terrible moment, they thought the old woman had fallen; but it turned out the twine was just caught on a rock.

At last, when it seemed they would break in two from

the strain, they saw a gray head appear above the low wall. Soon they saw two wizened hands grab at the stones; and finally a thin old woman, dressed in old-fashioned clothes, heaved herself over the wall onto the grass and safety.

Tad and Martha ran to the woman's side.

The old woman looked up into their faces, her blue eyes glistening with tears. "I know not from where you have come," she said, "but you have saved the life of old Granny Byram."

The twins looked into the old woman's face. She wasn't their grandmother, yet they saw right away that she had Byram eyes. Clear and blue, they were very much like their Great-aunt Ruth's and like their father's. They knew she could not be their "granny" but rather their great-grandmother many times over. They flung their arms around her and hugged her for all they were worth.

15

GRANNY BYRAM

"I am more convinced than ever," Granny Byram was telling Tad and Martha, "that I am simply getting too old to manage Bluebird Hall by myself. This tumble into the well is not the first accident I have had. Perhaps those who say that I am not fit to live alone are correct."

"What sort of accidents have you had?" asked Tad.

Granny Byram took another sip of tea before replying. Tad and Martha were seated across from her at the old familiar kitchen table.

"I have told no one else," she began, "but I feel as though I know you two. It is almost as if you were my grandchildren—not that I have any, mind you. But somehow I am convinced I can trust you, whoever you are, and despite your strange attire. Well, it all started last autumn. One day, I apparently left a large platter on the staircase. Coming downstairs later, I tripped over it and had a nasty fall. Fortunately, all I did was injure my knee slightly. It could have been much worse."

"But why would you leave a platter on the stairs?" asked Tad.

"That is perhaps the oddest part. I have no recollection of putting the platter there. In fact, it was a platter I cannot even recall having used for the longest time. And there have been times when I have put pies in the oven to bake—or so I thought—but later, when checking to see if they were properly done, I discovered I had not put them in the oven at all. And I have lit lamps in the middle of the day without having recalled I had done so. My great fear is that I shall do something to damage Bluebird Hall without realizing it. The other day, for example, I lit a fire in the living room fireplace. I was sure I had opened the flue. When I returned, the flue was tightly shut and the room was filled with smoke."

"Maybe it slipped shut by itself," suggested Tad. "I know that flue, it doesn't work terribly well."

Granny Byram gave Tad a sharp glance. "How do you know that?"

"It would be hard to explain," answered Tad. "Let's just say we're here to help you."

"Help is what I desperately need. If you two had not come along, I should still be imprisoned at the bottom of the well. The good Lord alone knows what might have become of me."

"Exactly how did you end up in the well?" Martha asked.

"I am not sure. I was standing near it, and then suddenly I felt myself flying through the air—almost as if someone had pushed me."

"Maybe someone did," said Tad.

"But there was no one around," replied the old woman, starting to cry.

After Tad and Martha had consoled her and her last tear seemed to have fallen, she suddenly burst out again: "And I have written to my son again and again, but he has not replied. I so fear something has happened to him, and I cannot continue to run this large house without him."

"Where is he?" asked Tad.

"My John shipped out on a whaling vessel over a year ago. The last I heard, he was somewhere near New-foundland. At first he sent me his wages every month. This was why he took the job, you see. It pays well, and we needed the money. But no news and no money have come for the longest time. That is not like John."

"Don't you have any other kids?" asked Martha.

"Kids?" said Granny Byram, who had never heard the word.

"She means 'children,'" explained Tad.

Granny Byram looked even sadder than before. "No," she said, "my daughter, Virginia, died two autumns ago of influenza. My husband died shortly after. Some say it was of influenza also, but I say it was of a broken heart. He so loved our daughter!" She dabbed at a tear, then went on. "Sometimes when I come into the living room, I can almost see him there, reading one of his precious books. I can almost hear him saying, just as he used to, 'Oh, Emma, my love, we may not have as much gold as our neighbors the Snivells, but we have a greater treasure. We have our love for one another, and we have the love of reading and fine books to read.'"

As she said this, Tad recalled that in the last century, books were much rarer than they are nowadays.

"No," continued Granny Byram with certainty, "unless John returns soon from the sea, I shall be obliged to sell Bluebird Hall."

"Sell Bluebird Hall?" gasped the twins. "But that's impossible!"

"Nothing," the old woman replied, "is impossible."

That afternoon, while Granny Byram napped, Tad and Martha did some investigating. They discovered that the year was 1849 and that Emma Byram was actually their great-great-great-great-great-grandmother.

"Good grief!" said Tad. "I bet this is the first time anybody's ever met their great-grandmother four times over, and in the same house where they still live."

"It also might be the last time."

"Meaning?"

"Meaning we'd better get busy and make sure Granny Byram doesn't sell Bluebird Hall; or when we get back to the future, we'll have no place to live."

"It's funny," Tad said, "how the house looks the same, yet different. It's so much quieter."

"Of course," agreed Martha. "There aren't any cars or radios or anything. And no pollution." Martha took a deep breath. "No wonder Tamburlaine wanted to keep things like this."

Approaching the well where they'd found their great-great-great-great-great-grandmother, Tad suddenly threw himself on the ground.

"Are you sick?" asked Martha.

"No, I'm looking for evidence. Don't interrupt my concentration."

"Evidence of what?" asked Martha, ignoring Tad's request.

"Look!" Tad called out a moment later. "I've found something!"

"What is it?"

Tad examined the object in his hand. "It looks like a bag of pipe tobacco," he answered. "And it doesn't look like it's been here long. Someone could have dropped it when they pushed Granny Byram into the well."

"But I still don't see why someone would want to do that to begin with," said Martha.

"Something tells me that that is what we've been sent here to find out."

"Granny Byram," Tad began at dinner that night, "Martha and I have some questions to ask you."

"And I have a few I should like to ask you," the old woman replied. "However, something tells me you might not wish to answer them."

"What makes you think that?" Martha wanted to know.

Granny Byram looked embarrassed. "It has been said in the family that I have second sight."

"Well," said Tad, "it's not that we wouldn't want to answer your questions. It's more that I'll bet you wouldn't believe our answers."

"I just might," replied Granny Byram. "I already know you arrived from nowhere just in time to rescue me, and that you found me with that magic star you carry."

"It's called a flashlight," said Tad.

"Whatever. Furthermore, although you have never

before set foot in Bluebird Hall, you know your way around the house as though you lived here."

Tad was about to attempt an explanation when Granny Byram continued. "Perhaps it does not matter. My heart tells me that you belong here. And it tells me just to accept your presence. So be it."

"You know," said Martha softly, "both of our grandmothers died before we were born. I always wondered what it would be like to have a grandmother. Now I know."

Resuming his questions, Tad asked if there was anybody in Rock Ridge who might especially wish to live in Bluebird Hall.

Granny Byram gave a hearty chuckle. "Is there anybody? How about everybody!"

"Everybody?" Tad repeated, confused. "What do you mean?"

"Perhaps I was exaggerating just a bit," Granny Byram replied. "Yet Bluebird Hall is known to be the loveliest house in Rock Ridge. It has the best well, and a good water supply is something money cannot buy. Also, it is located between town and the Post Road, a most convenient location. I can think of at least a dozen folk in Rock Ridge who have offered to buy Bluebird Hall, and some were quite insistent. I have always refused. I have always felt strong and capable. That is, until this last half year. Now, the idea of moving into a smaller cottage seems less impossible."

"But what happens when John comes back?"

"But what if he does not?" said Granny Byram. "I

curse the day I ever let him join the whaling trade. It is so dangerous a profession."

"Tell me this," said Tad. "Do any of the people who have their eyes on Bluebird Hall smoke a pipe?"

Granny Byram narrowed her blue eyes in thought. "There is but one," she answered, "and he happens to be the most persistent of the buyers. Also the wealthiest. Should I sell Bluebird Hall, I fear I might have to sell it to him. He would bully the others into foregoing the idea. Yes, he would dearly love to be the lord of Bluebird Hall."

"And just who is this pipe-smoking rich man?"

"Horatio Snivell," Granny Byram said.

16
THE LETTER

"Oh, those Snivells!" exclaimed Martha. "They're always up to no good, no matter which century they're in."

"Now, now," soothed Granny Byram, "I certainly have no love for the Snivells. A more reprehensible band of blowhards I have yet to encounter. However, I do not think they would stoop to illegality. They were, after all, great heroes during the Revolutionary War."

"Good grief!" Tad almost shouted. "They weren't heroes, they were traitors. And I should know, I was . . ." Then he paused.

"You were what?" asked Granny Byram in a low voice.

"It's a long story," said Tad lamely, brushing his short hair back against his head, they way he did when he couldn't think of anything else to do.

Tad and Martha decided to keep a secret watch on Bluebird Hall. They told Granny Byram to let no one know of their presence.

"That way," explained Tad, "no one will suspect we're watching the house."

"Who would believe me, anyway?" Granny Byram smiled. "Children from nowhere who seem to know everything. People would no longer say I was just getting old, they would say I had gone crazy."

It was mid-afternoon. With Tad and Martha's help, Granny Byram had prepared four pies, and the three had laughed and joked as they worked.

"I have not heard such laughter in this kitchen for many a long month," said Granny Byram.

Once the pies were in the brick oven, Granny Byram went upstairs to do some sewing. Tad and Martha set off to patrol. All through Bluebird Hall's long corridors and many rooms they went, marveling at how little their home had changed over the centuries. The living room, with windows on three sides, was still bathed in sunlight all day long, while the study, a small room with just one window, received a patch of light only during late afternoon.

"You know," said Martha, "maybe if we lose Bluebird Hall in the future, we could bring Mom and Joe back to the past and live with Granny Byram."

"That's not a bad idea."

The wonderful smell of baking pies wafted through Bluebird Hall, interrupting their thoughts.

"Hey," said Martha. "Let's go check the pies. Race you to the kitchen!"

They'd only been in the kitchen long enough to discover that the pies needed more time to bake when they heard soft footsteps approaching the house from the back, behind the kitchen.

"Quick!" said Tad. "Someone's coming."

"Granny Byram's upstairs. It's got to be someone else. People don't walk that quietly unless they're up to no good."

Sure enough, the footsteps were being made by someone determined to make as little noise as possible. And they were heading straight toward the kitchen door.

Swiftly, Tad and Martha darted under the kitchen table, adjusting the tablecloth so that no one could see they were there.

Someone was trying the door handle. Slowly, the door opened and the intruder entered the kitchen. Whoever it was went over to the brick oven. The twins heard the stranger heave a sigh of satisfaction.

Knowing the intruder was now occupied, the twins peeked out from under the tablecloth.

One pair of brown and one pair of blue eyes peered across the room. The expression in both pairs said, "Just as we thought."

The man at the stove was removing all four pies from the oven. He then placed them on the wooden counter at the far side of the room. Looking around nervously, but fortunately not seeing the twins, he left the kitchen, leaving the oven door open behind him.

Before smoke could fill the room, Tad raced over and closed the oven door.

"I'll say one thing about those Snivells," remarked Tad. "You can always recognize them."

* * *

"So thank the Lord I am not losing my faculties!" cried Granny Byram. "It was just that miserable Horatio Snivell trying to make me think I was."

To celebrate their discovery, Granny Byram decided to make a special dinner.

"And I shall do it myself," she announced. "You children have helped enough today. Go off and enjoy yourselves."

While Granny Byram cooked, Tad and Martha set off to really explore Bluebird Hall in the year 1849. Of course, they were partially in search of the treasure.

Both twins laughed to see how their own bedrooms had looked at the time and regretted the fact that they hadn't brought a camera.

After two hours of exploring turned up nothing even remotely resembling a treasure, the search party returned to the kitchen, where Granny Byram was putting the finishing touches on dinner.

"Tonight we shall eat in the dining room," she said.

They used the best silver, and it was the same silver they were still using on special occasions over a century later at Bluebird Hall. Amazingly, they even recognized the plates: handmade, handpainted ones that looked as though they belonged in a museum. Only one, a large platter, had survived to the present day. It was kept on a sideboard in the dining room and was never used. All the others had been broken or lost over the years.

It was a wonderful dinner—delicious meat from the smokehouse; the best Indian pudding Tad and Martha had ever tasted; and, to finish it off, the pies. Granny

Byram even offered them beer. It seemed everyone, including children, drank ale at the time. Tad and Martha took a sip, but only Martha liked it.

After dinner, they sat in the living room, and Granny Byram read to them from one of her husband's favorite books. Somehow the excitement of the day and the size of the meal left Tad and Martha exhausted. Before long, they were falling asleep in their chairs to the accompaniment of Granny Byram's soothing voice. The next thing they knew, they were up in their bedrooms, being tucked into soft, comfortable beds, feeling warm and cozy beneath brightly colored quilts.

"It's been a wonderful day," murmured Martha sleepily as Granny Byram kissed her good-night.

"Yes, that it has. And tomorrow shall be just as wonderful."

But she was wrong.

It was before lunch.

Granny Byram was in the back, tending her garden, and Tad and Martha were in the kitchen making sandwiches. Just as the last sandwich was made, hoofbeats sounded from Bluebird Hall's long, tree-lined drive.

Racing to the front door, the twins saw a man dismounting from a black horse. He drew an envelope out of a pouch.

Eyeing Tad and Martha oddly, the man asked, "Is this Bluebird Hall?"

"It is."

"And does Emma Byram live here?"

"She does."

"Then," continued the rider, "this letter is for her."

Handing Martha the letter, he remounted. With a sharp pull on the reins and a quick jab with his boots, the man soon had the horse galloping away down the long drive.

Granny Byram examined the letter with interest. "I cannot imagine who might have written this," she told the twins. "I do not recognize the handwriting. You see, the only person who ever writes me is my John, and this letter is not from him."

"So open it," Martha suggested impatiently.

Granny Byram paused.

"You do it, and read it to me," she said in a soft voice. "I know not why, but my heart tells me there is something terribly wrong."

Martha opened the stiff envelope and read the letter to herself. Her face fell; and for one of the few times in her life, she couldn't think of a word to say. In silence she handed Tad the letter.

When Tad had finished reading, he looked at Granny Byram. "It's not good news," he said quietly.

"Just read it to me," Granny Byram answered, putting an arm around Martha for support.

"It's from the New England Whaling Company," began Tad, "in Boston. It's dated last month." And Tad read her the contents of the letter.

Dear Mrs. Byram,

It is our sad duty to inform you that your son, John Byram, is lost at sea and presumed dead. His whaling vessel, *The Liberty*, went down in a gale off the Newfoundland coast with all hands aboard. The New England Whaling Company regrets this unfortunate news.

"It's signed, 'Timothy White,'" finished Tad in a shaky voice.

Granny Byram was just staring into space, her eyes open wide.

"My John, my John," she said at last. Then the tears started. It seemed as though they'd never stop. When they finally did, Tad and Martha made Granny Byram a strong cup of tea and tucked her into bed, staying with her until she'd cried herself to sleep. They then sat in the hall outside her bedroom, talking quietly.

"All this makes me miss Mom," said Martha. "It makes me want to go home."

"We *are* home," Tad replied.

"I mean, home in our own time," answered Martha, "where we belong. How do we get back there, anyhow?"

"I don't know," Tad admitted. "I guess it's up to Tamburlaine."

"Then he should let us go back just as soon as Granny Byram is feeling a little better."

"Maybe," said Tad in a small voice.

"What do you mean?" Martha asked.

"I mean, maybe Tamburlaine sent us back here to stay—forever. Mom still has Joe, but now Granny Byram has no one. Maybe it's up to us to stay here and grow up in the eighteen hundreds. Remember, Tamburlaine said we might find more than we expected. This could be it."

"But that's impossible!" cried Martha.

"No," replied Tad, "nothing is impossible."

17

THE DARK PASSAGE

Night had fallen on Bluebird Hall. Granny Byram had eaten a small dinner and gone back to bed. Martha stayed with her until she was asleep.

To fight off the chill of the spring evening in the silent house, Tad had built a fire in the living room fireplace. He and Martha were sitting on the floor in front of it, gazing into the flames and thinking about John Byram, lost at sea.

"I wish we could have met him," Martha said.

"He looked a lot like Dad," Tad added, remembering the portrait of her son that Granny Byram had shown them.

"Yes," said Martha sadly, the firelight turning her chestnut hair golden.

Suddenly, Tad burst out. "Good grief! This can't be right."

"Slow down," said Martha. "I have no idea what you're talking about."

Tad's brown eyes were aglow with excitement. "We

know Bluebird Hall has been in the Byram family since the seventeen hundreds, right?"

"Right."

"And we know it's always been handed down from father to son, right?"

"Right, though that seems unfair. What's wrong with handing it down to a daughter once in a while?"

"Nothing. That just wasn't the way they did things back then. Now it's different."

"Thank goodness," said Martha emphatically.

"Anyway," continued Tad, "since Bluebird Hall has always gone from father to son—or, let's say, from parent to child—then that means John Byram couldn't be dead."

"I don't get it."

"I mean that if he were dead, there'd be no one for Granny Byram to hand Bluebird Hall over to. And I know for a fact that it's always gone to a son, never to a cousin or anyone like that."

"So maybe Tamburlaine hasn't sent us here for good?"

"Right. I'll bet that letter was a fake, and I'll bet I know who faked it."

Martha's blue eyes grew round.

"Oh, that devil!" she said. "He's trying to make Granny Byram think her son's dead so she'll sell Bluebird Hall to him."

"Right. But we'd better move fast, or Granny'll sell Bluebird Hall and—"

"And," finished Martha, "when we get back to the future, we'll have nowhere to live!"

"Do you think she heard us?" whispered Tad as he and Martha slipped into the shadows of the trees surrounding Bluebird Hall.

"I don't think so," answered Martha, peering up at the dark house.

"I hope you're right."

"And I hope you know where we're going," said Martha, walking carefully in the darkness. "It's past midnight. I don't think we'll be able to ask anyone directions."

"Good grief! I've been here before, you know; and, believe me, I know where the Snivells live."

"But what are we going to do when we get there?"

"Investigate, of course," said Tad. "If the Snivells faked that letter, it stands to reason there might be some incriminating evidence in their house."

"But what if you're wrong?"

"That's why I didn't want to tell Granny Byram what we were up to tonight. I don't want to get her hopes up until we're sure."

An owl swooped overhead, and from nearby a wolf howled. Tad and Martha met no one as they found their way through the Rock Ridge of 1849.

Staying behind bushes and under trees as much as possible, the twins finally stood in front of Snivell Manor.

"Hey!" cried Martha. "I remember when they tore this place down. Dad took us to see it, remember?"

"You bet," Tad grinned. "And do you remember Dad

saying we should always try to remember exactly how it looked? I wonder if he knew somehow that we'd be seeing it again."

"Ooh," said Martha, shivering. "What a spooky thought."

Like shadows, the twins approached the sleeping house.

"Let's try the kitchen door," whispered Tad. "They used to keep it unlocked—back in the seventeen seventies, that is."

But the door was locked.

"What now?" asked Martha.

"I've got some old keys in my knapsack. Let's see," Tad said, fishing around. "Here they are. Locks were simpler then. One's got to work."

Producing a ring of old-fashioned keys, Tad set to work. At last his efforts were rewarded, and the twins heard the lock turn inside the door.

"Good work," whispered Martha as they entered the quiet house.

With the flashlight turned on its lowest strength, the two went straight to the study.

"Maybe we'll get lucky," said Tad. "Maybe what we're looking for will be in the secret drawer."

In the study, Martha tipped a chair against the door so they could not be surprised while searching. They also took the precaution of opening a window in case they had to escape quickly.

To Tad's disappointment, the secret drawer was empty.

"Maybe they forgot how to use it," he said, shaking his head.

"Forget the old drawer," ordered Martha. "Let's ransack the desk."

"Search, not ransack," said Tad, and the two set to work.

"I've never seen so many boring letters," complained Martha about twenty minutes later. "Old Horatio Snivell must be the—"

"Ssh!" interrupted Tad. "Did you hear something?"

A loud creak from the main staircase was answer enough.

"Quick, under the desk!" ordered Tad. "I'll move the chair and hide behind the curtains. Don't even breathe."

"I tell you, I heard something," a woman was saying. "Clear as day it was, and it was coming from your study."

"Now, now, Prudence," answered a man. "You know you are always hearing things. Just last week you—"

"I know nothing of the kind," interrupted the woman, "so keep silent, Horatio."

Pushing open the study door, the Snivells entered the room. They were both dressed in their night clothes. Mrs. Snivell, a scrawny woman with two long braids, was carrying a lantern, while her husband, the same man the twins had seen at Bluebird Hall, held a firearm.

"See, Prudence," he said, "empty."

"But I swear I heard something."

"Take a look," Mr. Snivell said, chuckling. "The window was left ajar. No doubt you heard the breeze rustling some papers on the desk. I shall shut it so we both can get some sleep."

Tad held his breath and tried to make his small body even smaller. Closer and closer to the window and the curtains where Tad was hiding came Mr. Snivell. Pressed tightly against the wall, Tad felt the man's arms brush against him as he reached to shut the window.

"I am positive I shut that window earlier tonight," insisted Prudence.

"Now, now dear. Let us just go back to bed and worry about it in the morning."

"But . . ." protested Prudence as her husband steered her out of the study and back up the stairs.

Out from behind the curtains, Tad put a finger to his lips and shook his head meaningfully. Martha knew his look meant, "Don't say a word." This wasn't easy for her. Still, by concentrating, she was able to keep silent as they continued their search of the desk.

"Now this," whispered Martha, "is really odd."

Tad took a look at the paper Martha was holding. He nodded in agreement and pocketed the paper.

"For evidence," he said.

It would make good evidence, indeed. How could Mr. Snivell possibly explain why he had blank stationery in his desk from the New England Whaling Company?

"That letter *was* a fake," whispered Tad as he and Martha headed back to the kitchen. Tiptoeing toward the door, Tad suddenly felt hands grabbing his arm. His heart skipped a beat. Then he realized it was Martha. "What—" he began as Martha pointed to the kitchen door. For an instant, the twins stood frozen in place.

Someone was at the kitchen door. Tad switched off the flashlight. The man at the door kept knocking. "Horatio," he shouted, "It's William. Answer the door!"

Before they knew where to run, Tad and Martha heard footsteps descending the stairs. The stairs opened on to the hall just beyond the kitchen. The twins were now trapped in the kitchen. In the darkness, they tried to find a decent hiding place.

"Under the table," whispered Martha. But there were too many chairs, and it would have been too noisy to move them.

Wheeling around, Tad saw two closed doors on the far side of the kitchen. One, as he knew only too well, was the larder door. Not wanting to be trapped in there a second time, Tad dashed over and tried the other door. It was open. Just inside was a staircase, leading down.

"Quick!" called Tad. "In here. There's got to be a place to hide in the basement."

Just in time, the twins shut the door behind them as Mr. Snivell entered the kitchen.

"What is it, what is it?" they heard him demand grumpily.

"It is your neighbor William. I thought I saw strange lights moving about in your house."

"You are as loony as my wife," Mr. Snivell retorted. "It was only Prudence and I, carrying a lantern and looking around as she thought she had heard noises."

"I meant not to trouble you," the neighbor answered. "But better safe than sorry."

"So they say," barked back Mr. Snivell, shutting the door firmly in his neighbor's face.

In the basement below, Tad and Martha waited in hushed silence until they heard Mr. Snivell take himself back upstairs to bed.

"Good grief!" said Tad. "That was close. Let's get out of here."

At the foot of the basement stairs, Martha suddenly halted.

Tilting her head slightly to one side and brushing her hair behind her right ear, Martha cupped her hand to hear more clearly.

"What is it?" whispered Tad.

"I'm not sure. It sounds like tapping."

"I hear it, too," said Tad. "It's probably water dripping or something. C'mon, let's get out of here."

Tad was already halfway up the stairs before he realized Martha was not following him.

"Martha! C'mon."

"It's not water. It's too regular, like a code or something."

Back down the stairs went Tad. Standing next to Martha, he listened again.

"You're right. That does sound like some sort of code."

"Then where's it coming from?"

Tad turned his flashlight up in strength and surveyed the Snivells' basement. There were trunks piled up in one corner, a table with a few broken chairs in another, and some torn blankets heaped by a third. The walls had a stray picture here and there, as well as a built-in bookcase.

Following their ears, Tad and Martha ended up next to the bookcase.

"The tapping is coming from here," said Martha, confused. "But how—"

"Wait a minute!" said Tad. "Remember Great-aunt Ruth's house? That bookcase she has? It hides a secret staircase. A lot of Colonial homes had them. Let's find a way to get it open."

By pushing aside some books on the top shelf, the twins were able to uncover a hidden handle. When pulled, this flipped open a latch, and the left side of the bookcase inched away from the wall. The twins pulled the bookcase open and found themselves staring down a narrow, dark passageway.

The tapping noises were coming from somewhere in the passage.

"After you," said Tad nervously.

"You're the one with the flashlight," said Martha. "You go first."

It was damp and musty in the passage, moss was even growing on the walls.

The passage made a sharp left turn, and the twins unexpectedly found themselves face-to-face with a door. Made of thick wood, it was bolted shut from the outside.

Putting his ear to the door, Tad listened. Then he nodded his head.

"The noises are coming from in there," he said.

Without stopping to think, Tad and Martha undid the bolts and threw open the door. Tad shone his flashlight in, while he and Martha took a good look.

They saw a small, square room with rough stone walls and a dirt floor. On the floor was a dirty mat. On the mat, bound at wrists and ankles, was a young man.

The moment the light fell on his face, Tad and Martha knew who he was.

18

RIDDLES

"Release me, you scoundrels!" cried John Byram.

"We're here to rescue you," said Tad as he and Martha rushed to the man's side.

"Then be quick about it, for the love of God!"

Fingers flew, and soon the ropes around John's wrists and ankles lay on the dirt floor.

It was startling how much John Byram looked like the twins' father—and Joe, too, even down to his hot temper. Of course, his hair was a good deal longer than their father's had ever been; but except for that, the two men could easily have passed for brothers.

John Byram leaped to his feet.

"Hurry!" he shouted. "I know not what may happen next, but I fear I am to be press-ganged."

"Press what?"

"Press-ganged—forced to work on a ship," John explained quickly. "Although it be illegal, it happens nonetheless. Why else would I be kept prisoner? I do not even know where I am."

"You're in Rock Ridge," Tad told him, "and in the basement of—"

"Tell him later," urged Martha. "Let's get out of here before you-know-who shows up with his rifle."

"Sound reasoning," agreed John. "Show me the way with that mighty lantern of yours."

Soon they had left the damp passageway and were at the foot of the stairs leading up to the kitchen. John Byram was just about to start up the stairs when a whiny voice sounded from the top.

"I tell you, Horatio, I heard voices in the basement."

"Now, Prudence, it is but your imagination."

"Well then, if you will not look, then I shall."

"All right, I shall go. Stand aside, dear."

As the twins and John Byram watched in horror, the door at the top of the stairs opened and through it stepped Horatio Snivell. He had a lantern in one hand and a firearm in the other.

He caught sight of John Byram at the same instant John Byram saw him.

"Horatio Snivell, you conniving snake! So it was you who kept me here."

"Silence, Byram!" commanded Snivell, putting down his lantern. He descended the stairs, his weapon aimed steadily at John Byram's heart.

Suddenly, Martha gave a piercing shriek. Anyone else would have thought her to be in deep anguish; only Tad realized she was just providing an important distraction. Taking advantage of it, Tad darted forward and beamed his flashlight directly into Mr. Snivell's eyes.

Momentarily blinded, Snivell reached up automatically to shield his eyes, lost his balance on the stairs, and stumbled downward.

At that moment, John Byram leaped at Mr. Snivell and pulled him forward. Mr. Snivell fell heavily down the wooden stairs, landing at the bottom with a loud thud. Before he could struggle to his feet, John Byram had grabbed his gun and was now pointing it at Mr. Snivell's heaving chest.

"Fetch the ropes," he commanded. When Martha returned with them, John Byram handed her the gun and began tying up Mr. Snivell with strong sailor knots.

Prudence Snivell appeared in the kitchen doorway and saw her husband bound and a girl with a gun.

"Oh, my stars!" she moaned, and fainted dead away.

"What'll we do with them?" asked Martha when Mr. Snivell was completely trussed up.

"We could lock them in the room in which I was held," said John, "yet that damp pit is too inhumane a jail even for the Snivells."

"I've got it!" said Tad. "The larder. It's got a thick door and a strong lock, and it's nice and dry. Believe me, I should know."

Soon a fuming Horatio and a revived but still confused Prudence were securely shut in the larder.

"Serves them right," said Tad, forgetting that it wasn't this Mr. Snivell but actually his great-grandfather who had locked up Tad.

John knew who in town to tell about Mr. Snivell's activities and his current imprisonment. "I'll see to it later," he said as he and the twins headed straight for Bluebird Hall. They'd decided John would save his story until he could tell it to his mother, Tad, and Martha all at once.

"I am sure my mother will be glad to see me," John said as the three raced along Bluebird Hall's tree-lined drive.

"That's putting it mildly," Tad answered. "She got a letter today saying you were dead."

"What?" John cried.

"That's why we investigated," put in Martha.

"I shall be wanting to hear more about you two later," John said. "Never before have two strangers looked so familiar, not to mention your odd dress and the mighty lantern you carry. I want to know all."

It was decided that Tad and Martha would wake Granny Byram, telling her they had good news about her son. Then they would call for him to enter.

"If she believes me dead, seeing me unannounced might be too great a shock," John had said.

So, up in Granny Byram's room, Martha gently shook the sleeping woman's shoulder, while Tad lit a few lamps.

"What is it?" said Emma, a frightened look darkening her blue eyes.

"It's good news. In fact, it's wonderful news," cried Martha. "That letter was a fake. Your son wasn't drowned, he's alive. And he's right here."

At that moment, the door opened. John and his mother were soon locked in a tearful embrace.

"Oh, my son, my treasure!" Old Mrs. Byram was weeping. "I thought I had lost you forever."

"No, I am here," her son answered, also weeping. "And I am never going to leave again."

Tiptoeing out so John and his mother could be reunited in private, Tad and Martha went down to the kitchen and sat around the familiar wooden table.

"I just can't believe it," Martha was saying.

"You can't believe what?"

"That that man upstairs is really our great-great-great-great-grandfather. He looks even younger than Mom."

"And boy, does he ever look like Dad," Tad added. "It sure makes me miss him."

"Me, too," said Martha, giving her brother's hand a soft pat.

"Many was the time I wrote you, Mother," John Byram said over breakfast the following morning. The kitchen at Bluebird Hall was bathed in sunlight, and Tad, Martha, and Granny Byram were listening at last to John's story.

"Yet I never received a letter for the longest time," Granny Byram replied. "How is that possible?"

"Sounds as though somebody was swiping them," said Tad. "Who's in charge of the mail around here?"

"Is not the postmistress none other than Prudence Snivell?" cried John.

"So it is," said Granny Byram.

"I had written you," continued John, "saying that I was leaving the ship and would be arriving back in Rock Ridge by the evening coach on Tuesday of last week. Lo and behold, when I arrived in Greenvale, a small carriage was awaiting me. The driver, a man I did not recognize, informed me that you had sent it to collect me. Never suspecting, I got in; and before I could fight my way out, I was knocked on the head. The next thing I knew, I awoke in that small, musty prison where Tad and Martha found me. I never even knew where I was, or by whom I had been captured."

"That," said Tad, "was exactly the way they wanted it."

"What do you mean?" asked Granny Byram.

"I mean that Mr. Snivell wanted you to think John was dead so you would sell Bluebird Hall," said Tad. "Then, once it was sold, Mr. Snivell would have released John without his ever knowing who had been holding him captive."

"That makes sense," John said. "And it is what I shall tell the authorities directly after breakfast."

"But why would someone go to such trouble to get Bluebird Hall?" asked Martha.

"I can explain that," Granny Byram said. "It is not just that Bluebird Hall has the best well and the best location in Rock Ridge—much preferable to Snivell Manor. But it has also long been said that some Byram buried a treasure in Bluebird Hall. Mr. Snivell is such a greedy creature, I have no doubt he believed these legends."

"But is there a treasure?" asked Tad.

Both Granny Byram and John started to chuckle.

"Goodness no."

"No truth in it whatsoever."

Tad and Martha did their best not to look too disappointed.

"I must go," said John. "Then, when I return, there is something else of importance I should like to do."

"What's that?" Martha wanted to know.

"I wish to hear everything there is to know about you two," John said with a smile.

"No treasure," sighed Martha later that morning. "What a waste."

"Not exactly, Martha. After all, we did rescue Granny Byram and John. And if we hadn't saved Bluebird Hall in eighteen forty-nine, it wouldn't be there for us in our own time."

"That's true," agreed Martha. "But don't you still wish we'd found a real treasure?"

"I guess so," answered Tad. "Who wouldn't?"

John returned before lunch, whistling to himself because Mr. Snivell really seemed to be in trouble. He and the twins then set out for a stroll around Bluebird Hall. Tad and Martha hadn't had so much fun with a grownup since their father died. John regaled them with breathtaking tales of his adventures at sea. It was impossible to believe that, back in their own time, John Byram was already dead for at least a century.

"Lunch," called Granny Byram from the kitchen.

Sitting down around the dining room table, the four Byrams were soon eating and talking as though they'd known one another always.

Tad and Martha had agreed they would tell John and his mother the entire truth about themselves.

"The worst they could do," Tad had said, "is not believe us. Yet somehow I think they will."

After the first course was over, John Byram said, "Let us clear the table. Then, over tea, we shall hear Tad and Martha's story. Something tells me it shall be a remarkable one. In fact, I have half a mind to fetch a friend of mine to hear it. No one loves stories the way he does."

"Who do you mean, dear?" asked Granny Byram.

"Tamburlaine, of course," replied John.

"Tamburlaine Firshadow?" Tad and Martha stopped on their way to the kitchen, their plates still in their hands.

"Good grief!" said Tad. "You mean you know him, too?"

"Certainly I do," replied John. "Evidently, you do also."

"You bet," said Martha. "In fact, that's why we're here."

"Then let's get the table cleared so we can hear all about it," said John.

Behind Granny Byram, Tad and Martha hurried through the door between the dining room and the kitchen.

"What do you have there?" a voice asked.

"The plates, of course," replied Martha, not yet realizing whose voice it was.

"Mom!" burst out Tad. "What are you doing here?"

Standing in the kitchen was not Granny Byram but their own mother.

"What am I doing here?" said their mother. "I live here."

Looking around in confusion, Tad and Martha quickly saw they were back in the present.

"What the—" began Martha when their mother interrupted.

"What lovely plates," she said. "You know, I believe they match that large platter. Wherever did you get them?"

Tad thought quickly. "We found them in the big attic," he said.

Without warning, their mother started crying softly.

"Mom, what's the matter?" asked Martha. "Did we do something wrong?"

"Of course not, dear, not at all. It's just that it was so sweet of you to bring me these plates, and just when I needed some cheering up. I'll bet they're almost as old as the house. Even if we have to leave Bluebird Hall, at least we'll be bringing parts of it away with us when we go."

Bluebird Hall in the present was an unhappy place in which to come back. No bank had approved a loan, and the Byrams were running out of time. It was a glum bunch who sat around after supper that evening. Even a fire in the fireplace did little to raise their spirits.

"Mom," said Tad, trying to think of something interesting to discuss, "did you ever hear of a relative of ours named Emma Byram?"

"Emma. Of course," their mother replied without even pausing. "And she had a son, John, I believe."

"That's right," said Martha. "What do you know about them?"

"It's funny you should ask. In fact, I can't believe your father and I never mentioned them to you. You see, they lived back in the eighteen hundreds. They both had a reputation for being a little, well, a little unusual."

"In what way?" asked Joe, looking up from a sports magazine.

"It's an odd story; but one day, when your father was doing some research in the Historical Society archives, he came across a diary written by a neighbor back in the eighteen fifties. This neighbor wrote that a lot of folks in Rock Ridge thought Emma and John were a bit strange. It seems both of them claimed that two children had come from nowhere, saved their lives, and then vanished into thin air."

"Good grief," said Tad, winking at Martha, "what a story."

"And that's not all," said their mother. "Your father was so taken with this story and the idea of the two mystery children that he never forgot it. So, shortly after, when you two were born, we named you after these two children. The neighbor had even written down the names Emma called them—Tad and Martha."

"Wow!" said Martha quietly. "I was named after myself!"

19

THE MISTS OF TIME

"The bank has given us a ten-day extension," Mrs. Byram was saying the next morning. "Not that I expect it to do us much good; no one's going to lend me any money, that's for sure."

"When's the new deadline?" asked Tad.

"December first."

"That's great," said Tad.

"All right," chimed in Martha.

"Calm down, children. It's just an extension, not a promise of more money," Mrs. Byram reminded them.

"Don't listen to them," Joe said. "They've been acting crazy for months now."

"All our problems are solved," cheered Tad when he and Martha had a chance to talk privately. "On December first we get a whole new set of wishes."

"Yes," Martha cried, "I knew it was my destiny to save Bluebird Hall. No matter the danger, no matter the—"

"No matter the situation, you talk too much," said Tad. "But seriously, we've got to figure out exactly what we're going to ask for. We've only got this one chance, or those Snivells will be moving into Bluebird Hall—and we know what slippery sneaks they are. You know I checked the Rock Ridge police records for eighteen forty-nine, and there was no mention anywhere of them getting into trouble for kidnapping John and terrorizing poor Emma. They must have bribed someone. Something tells me we're going to have to be pretty smart to outsmart them!"

"Why don't we ask Tamburlaine?"

"Good idea. If anyone can help us work our wishes right, it has to be Tamburlaine. And I'd like to hear more about John Byram."

Martha became very quiet.

"Tad," she said, "maybe we should try doing something for Tamburlaine this time."

"Such as?"

"Such as bringing Joe along. What do you say?"

"It's worth a try."

They found Joe in his room, kicking around some junk in his closet.

"I'm going through my stuff," he said hopelessly. "There's no way Mom can pay back that loan. I might as well get a headstart on packing," he continued, giving a box at his feet a swift kick. "Let's face it, we're going to end up crammed into some tiny apartment or something."

"Not necessarily," began Tad. "Listen, Joe. You know how you're always saying that Martha and I have been acting strange? Well—"

"Well, forget it," said Joe. "Maybe Mom's right, maybe we do fight too much. Just forget I ever said it."

"But you were right," insisted Tad.

"I was?"

"You bet," said Tad. "Wasn't he, Martha?"

"Very right," agreed Martha. "Very *very* right."

"But—"

"Anyway," Tad went on, "it's kind of hard to explain, but Martha and I would like to show you something pretty amazing. All you have to do is try to believe us. Okay?"

Joe's eyes narrowed. "Is this some kind of trick?"

"Pledge of honor," vowed both Tad and Martha.

"Well . . . " said Joe, wavering.

"Come on," pleaded Martha. "Just come with us. You'll be glad you did."

"You sound like a TV commercial," Joe teased her. But he got up anyway to join his brother and sister.

"Not this basement business again," said Joe, looking disgusted. "Haven't we already been through this?"

It was a cold afternoon, almost Thanksgiving, and the three of them stood shivering outside the Seven Willows Condominium.

"C'mon, Joe," begged Tad. "It's too cold to stand around arguing. You've come this far, why not come inside, too?"

127

"All right," muttered Joe. "But you'd better not be fooling around."

I hope it's there, I hope it's there, Martha prayed to herself as they entered the basement.

Standing in front of the wall with the NO STORAGE HERE sign on it, Tad and Martha each took one of Joe's hands.

That way, Tad had reasoned earlier, even if Joe sends out not-believing thoughts, his and Martha's thoughts would be on the outside, so maybe Joe's wouldn't get through.

"Hmmm," Martha had replied. "That has to be the least scientific thing you've ever said, but anything is worth a try."

So there they stood, in front of the wall, waiting. Joe was just beginning to squirm and make I-told-you-so noises when suddenly his eyes opened wide.

"Holy cow," he whispered.

As soon as the door materialized, the three were ushered into Tamburlaine's home.

The fox was on the sofa, the white owl was perched on Tamburlaine's shoulder—but something was different.

Something was wrong.

Martha felt it the instant she looked into Tamburlaine's eyes. They were now the color of mist, with a lost look in them.

Tad suspected something, too, when he looked out one of the windows. For one hundred feet or so, the view was clear as day. Then, it was as if a curtain had dropped; he could see no farther. Tamburlaine's land was lost in a thick gray fog.

Joe, meanwhile, was amazed by everything, exactly the way Tad had been on his first visit.

Gesturing for the Byrams to sit down, Tamburlaine remained silent.

It was Joe who spoke first. "How can there be country-side in the middle of Rock Ridge?" Then, turning to Tad and Martha, he said "So there was something here."

"Joe, welcome," said Tamburlaine in a faltering voice. "I have long hoped you would come . . . but . . ."

"Tamburlaine, what is it?" said Martha, for even the fox was rigid with fear, while the white owl made an occasional nervous circle around the room, almost as if it were trying to escape.

Settling his thin form in the chair opposite the sofa where Tad, Martha, and Joe were sitting, Tamburlaine held out his hands in front of him by way of answer.

At first, the only thing the children noticed were his long, strong-looking fingers. Then Tad saw what was not there.

"Tamburlaine," he whispered, "your ring. Where is it?"

Resting his hands on his knees, Tamburlaine said simply, "It has gone."

"Where'd it go?" Tad asked.

Tamburlaine smiled gravely. "These rings have minds of their own," he began. "I have never been sure whether we wear them or they wear us. You see, I was on a journey to the far reaches of my land, where different time zones have their shifting borders. It is a dangerous place, one where time and magic are very strong. When I returned home, I saw too late that my ring was no longer on my finger. I can only conclude it wished to remain in this no-man's land. Perhaps it had work of its own that needed doing."

"But can't you go back and get it?" asked Martha. "We'd help you."

"You bet," said Tad.

Even Joe, still confused, nodded agreement.

"Thank you, but it would be like looking for a shadow at midnight. It could be anywhere or everywhere but really nowhere at all."

"But what does all this mean?" Martha asked, almost afraid to hear the answer.

Tamburlaine bowed his head. "It was the power of the ring that created this shadow land, and it was the power of the ring that kept alive all life within it. With the ring gone, this land—and all within it—will gradually fade into the mists of time and vanish."

"Forever?" said Tad.

"Yes, forever, except in memory."

"And you along with it?" said Martha.

"I am ready to go," Tamburlaine replied. "I do not fear the mist. Yet I do grieve for the land. It is unlikely that Earth shall ever again be as fair as it is here. So," he continued, "you have come just in time to say farewell; I am glad of that."

The four fell into silence, silence inside the cabin and silence in the misty world outside, where no bird called and no human voice disturbed the immense quiet.

No one knew what to say until, suddenly, Tad leaped to his feet.

"Our rings!" he cried. "The one Martha found and the one I got from Mr. Snivell. You could combine them."

"Thank you, Tad," Tamburlaine said, smiling. "Yes, I could attempt combining those two and forging another ring of power as I did before. There are, you see, strict rules guiding the use of these rings, and one is that I could not ask you for yours. You must instead have offered it as, indeed, you just did.

"However, before you relinquish your ring, I must tell you that when you do and I combine the two into one, the door from my world to yours—that is, the door in the basement of this building—will vanish forever. There may be other doors, there may not. It will be up to you to find them should they exist. But never again will you be able to find my land and me by this route."

"But we may never see you again!" Martha burst out.

"You may not," Tamburlaine answered softly. "Now, there is a second thing you must know. Should you decide to relinquish your ring, I would need it this very moment. Next week or the week after would be too late. The land and I would be long gone."

"That's okay," said Martha impulsively. "Take it."

Tad, however, understood what Tamburlaine was saying.

"Marth," he said, "if we give up the ring right away, we won't get another chance to wish with it. We won't be able to save Bluebird Hall."

Martha turned pale.

"You two must decide," Tamburlaine told them

gently. "And believe me, whatever you decide will be right. There can be more than one right answer in this world. Now, I shall take Joe for a walk around the Field of the Seven Willows and leave you two to make up your minds. You must do it for yourselves. I cannot do it for you."

Taking Joe by the arm, Tamburlaine Firshadow left the room.

20

THE FIGURE IN THE MIST

It was the figure in the mist that helped Tad and Martha make up their minds. The odd thing, though, was that neither knew what the other had seen until much later. They'd been sitting on the windowsill when each one saw it, and each one knew what the decision had to be. After a minute or so of silence, they both spoke at the same time: "We've got to give our ring to Tamburlaine."

Tamburlaine and Joe soon returned from their walk, with Joe looking almost like a different person.

Tamburlaine received the ring and then asked Tad, Martha, and Joe to collect enough wood for a large fire. He disappeared for a moment into the mist, returning with a collection of herbs. Soon a fire was raging and a large black cauldron filled with water was bubbling on it. Tamburlaine then threw the herbs into the steaming water one by one. Looking at Tad and Martha, Tamburlaine said, "You know, it is a blessing in more ways than one that you brought Joe with you. It is part of the old magic that anyone performing this rite has to be assisted by three people—three being a powerful number, as you perhaps know."

Tamburlaine gave one ring to Tad and one to Martha. "You must send them on their way, giving them your blessings," he told them.

This they did, although it was very hard.

Tamburlaine then removed the string of beads with the small silver vial attached to it from around his neck. Very carefully, he opened the vial and poured its contents into his palm. It looked like gray dust yet seemed to sparkle oddly, even though there was no sunlight to reflect.

"This," Tamburlaine said softly, "is the last of the powder my father created. I hope enough remains to do the task."

Placing his right hand over his heart, Tamburlaine emptied the powder into the cauldron with his left. After watching it dissolve into the bubbling water, he gazed toward the sky with a faraway look. He then sat down in silence, his long legs crossed. Tad, Martha, and Joe joined him. The owl seemed to bow its head in prayer.

Every so often, Tamburlaine would recite something in an unknown language. Even though they could make no sense of the words, Tad, Martha, and Joe somehow felt it was the most beautiful thing they'd ever heard.

It could have been an hour later, it could have been

ten, when a column of smoke started rising from the cauldron straight into the air. It never shifted direction or changed form until it rose to a height of nearly one hundred feet. Perpendicular to earth and straight as a line, it hovered above the cauldron, changing color as time went on. At first blue-gray, it became darker and darker until it was an ominous midnight black. Then, like dawn after night, streaks of color flashed across it until, at long last, the streaks started changing from a rich, velvety purple to a light blue. Then it either vanished or just blended in with the sky, which was suddenly the same color.

The mist had cleared and Tamburlaine's land was glistening in the newborn light.

Looking into the cauldron, they found the water had boiled away. Then, with a pure sound like the ringing of a church bell, the cauldron itself split into pieces, its sides falling away from its bottom. There, on the bottom, lay the ring.

Tad and Martha recognized it as being almost identical to the one Tamburlaine had lost. Joe just thought it was strangely beautiful.

Though Tad thought the ring would be too scalding hot to touch, Tamburlaine reached down, took it, and placed it on the ring finger of his left hand. He then held it out for the three to admire. Martha, who could never hold herself back, reached out to touch it. It was as cool as the water in a deep lake.

"There is no more to say," Tamburlaine said softly, "except that you must go. A new magic has been created, and the old door to your world is rapidly losing its power. You must go quickly, or you will never be able to leave."

At the door, after they all had embraced, Martha couldn't help but cry out, "Tamburlaine, will we ever see you again?"

"People who find magic once," he replied, "often find it again."

Then the three found themselves ushered through the waiting door, which was growing fainter by the second. It was a difficult passage, like driving too quickly along a very bumpy road. In fact, the force propelling them through the door was so rough and they arrived back so suddenly that they were thrown to the floor of the dingy storage room.

"Let's get out of here," said Martha.

She took her brothers' hands, and they headed back to Bluebird Hall.

"I don't care about the extension," their mother said when they arrived home. She was so upset that she was really talking to herself. In fact, she had barely looked up from her desk, where she was sorting bills. "There's just no way I can raise the money. We might as well take the time to start packing carefully and to try and find a decent place to . . ."

Then she stopped and looked carefully at Tad, Martha, and Joe.

"It's the strangest thing," she said, "but the three of you look . . . I feel different just looking at you. Your father had a certain look that could calm me down no matter what was wrong. And you three look exactly the way he used to." She paused, and looked again at Tad, Martha, and Joe. "And you're all together," she added, "not fighting, but really together. I can feel it. Maybe it doesn't matter about the house as long as we're really together."

Tears in her eyes, Margaret Byram hugged all three children at once.

That night, Tad, Martha, and Joe met in the small attic. They each had something they wanted to say.

"It's about what I saw in the mist," began Martha. "I know you're going to think I'm overdramatizing, but I really did see—"

"I know you did, Marth," interrupted Tad, "because I saw, too."

Joe was the last to speak.

"I was afraid to believe it," he told them, "but when Tamburlaine took me for a walk, I saw someone there, standing nearby. He was just leaning against a tree, the way he always used to, looking happily at us."

"That's the way I saw him!" cried Martha.

"Me, too," said Tad. "Just like that."

"You know," said Martha softly, "I've always wanted to see Dad again. Not like the last time we saw him, in the hospital, but the way he really was. And now I have."

"Well," Joe began, "I didn't just see Dad, I spoke with him, too."

"What did he say?" cried Tad and Martha at once.

Joe looked down before speaking. "He said I didn't have to be so mad anymore, that things were all right. I never told anybody, but the day of Dad's accident, he and I had an argument. I got really mad at him. And then I never got the chance to speak to him again. And I never knew what to do about it. But now I feel different, a whole lot different."

21

THE FLIGHT OF THE OWL

"Today's the day," Mrs. Byram told Tad, Martha, and Joe. "We're going to go through the house from top to bottom. We've got to figure out what should be kept, what needs to be thrown out, and what might be given to charity."

"How about if we sold everything in Bluebird Hall?" Martha suggested. "Wouldn't that raise enough money?"

"Our old furniture is mostly antiques," Mrs. Byram said sadly, "but not the kind people pay a lot of money for. Ours is just too lived-in, I'm afraid."

"But there's got to be something—" said Tad when Joe broke in.

"Couldn't we just sell off some of the land? Then we'd still have the house."

"Some of Bluebird Hall's land was sold off in the last century," their mother said. "Current zoning laws don't allow that."

The four fell into silence. Mrs. Byram was blinking her eyes a lot, trying not to cry.

It was a Saturday morning, the day after they had left Tamburlaine behind forever. The three of them— especially Tad and Martha—now had two things to feel sad about.

"First we lose Tamburlaine and then our house. It's just not fair," Martha kept muttering.

"What did you say, dear?"

"Oh, nothing, Mom. I was just thinking out loud."

"Mom," Tad asked, "have you found a place for us to move?"

"There are two apartments in town currently available. I guess we could see them some afternoon next week, though I suppose it would have to be before Thursday, since that's Thanksgiving."

"I don't think I feel very thankful this year," grumbled Martha.

"Now, now," said Mrs. Byram.

Tad, Martha, and Joe were just setting off for the large attic to do some cleaning and packing, and Mrs. Byram was going into the study to make some appointments with realty agents, when the doorbell rang.

Before anyone could answer it, the door opened and in stepped Mr. Snivell. "Hi, folks," he said cheerily, though not nicely.

"Do you always enter other people's homes without permission?" Mrs. Byram asked coldly.

"Well," said Mr. Snivell, arching an eyebrow, "your home is my home. At least it will be soon!"

"Not until December!" said Tad.

"So get out until then," added Martha.

"Martha," said Mrs. Byram, "no matter what your private opinions, that is no way to treat a guest."

"That's for sure," Joe burst out. "It's too good for him!"

Mr. Snivell seemed to be enjoying himself so much that he ignored their remarks. "Actually," he said, "I am here with an offer."

"Namely?"

"This coming Thursday is, of course, Thanksgiving; and Mrs. Snivell and I would very much like to celebrate in our new home. If you would have everything ready for the movers by, let's say, Tuesday, I would be prepared to pay your moving expenses. How does that sound?"

"I do not wish to accept anyone's charity," replied Mrs. Byram, "especially yours."

"And you wouldn't be able to move in in one day, anyway," added Tad, sensible as ever.

"Of course not. We would simply send over the dining room table and chairs and a few hot trays. Our servants would prepare the meal at home and then bring it over for our guests and ourselves to enjoy here at Snivell Hall."

"Snivell Hall!" cried Tad, Martha, and Joe all at once.

"Why, you—" began Martha when her mother interrupted in a subdued voice. "Fine," she said to Mr. Snivell. "Provided the apartments I'm considering are still available, we'll be ready to have our possessions moved by Tuesday afternoon. Why draw it out? We have to move some time. And we might as well have it paid for. Hiring a moving van is terribly costly."

"Very wise, Mrs. Byram." Mr. Snivell smiled, rubbing his small, plump hands together in tiny, rapid motions. "At noon on Monday I shall return with my lawyer to sign this new agreement. I shall also instruct a representative of a local moving firm to appear that afternoon to receive your initial instructions. This gives you Monday morning to confirm your choice of which apartment you wish to take. Good day, I'll see myself out."

"But, Mom—" began Martha as Mr. Snivell disappeared through Bluebird Hall's front door.

"I don't want to talk about it," answered Mrs. Byram, tears welling in her eyes. "Just go and start packing!" she added, running from the hallway.

"Good grief!" Tad was saying. "I can see why we never came here much."

Brooms, large garbage bags, and cardboard boxes in hand, Tad, Martha, and Joe had just finished cleaning the big attic. Aside from a lifetime supply of dust and cobwebs, a broken chair, and part of a picture frame, the three had uncovered nothing.

"Let's take a break," suggested Joe. "I feel as though we've been at this for hours."

"That's for sure," agreed Martha. "I don't know how we'll ever get the whole house done by Tuesday."

"I don't even want to think about next week," Tad said solemnly. "Someone else is going to live here, in *our* home."

He pointed out through the small, diamond-shaped window at the near end of the room, just below the point where the two angles of the roof met. "Just look," he said. "That's the field where we found the ring, and that's the yard where we used to play, and that's—"

"That's coming right toward us," cried Martha.

Looking out of the attic window they saw a large white blur soaring above the far end of the field, heading directly toward them.

"Good grief, what is it?" said Tad. "It looks like—"

"Duck!" yelled Joe, shoving his sister and brother away from the window, for, at that moment, whatever it was came crashing through it. Slivers of glass and splinters of wood flew everywhere.

At first it seemed that a streak of light glowed in the gloom of the attic; but once inside the room, it slowed down enough so that it was at last identifiable.

It was Tamburlaine's white owl.

Once it had completed a low, swooping circle through the long, rectangular room, it gave its wings a mighty flap. Increasing speed, it flew back through the broken window.

"What the . . . " began Joe.

"How the . . . " added Tad.

Martha was plain speechless.

Upon the owl's exit, the window it had shattered flew up from the floor and rejoined itself piece by piece, exactly like a movie shown backward.

"You can't even tell it was ever broken," said Tad.

"But then why did it come?" Joe asked.

"Just look over there," said Martha, pointing toward the far end of the attic.

Lying delicately on the ground, almost shining in the attic's faint light, lay a single white feather.

Tad, Martha, and Joe raced over to examine it. For the first time, they noticed some odd cracks in the attic's wooden floor just under where the feather lay.

"Wait a second!" cried Tad. "Look, they form a square."

Joe gave a low whistle.

"It's a trap door," Martha exclaimed.

Producing his Swiss Army knife, Tad was able to lift the wooden square up from the floor.

Three faces looked down expectantly.

They saw a square cavity about a foot and a half in depth, and even dustier than the attic had been. It had a strangely pleasant, musty odor. Lying on the bottom was a package, carefully wrapped in now-shredded cloth.

"This must be it," said Martha with a flourish.

"This must be what?" asked Joe.

"The missing treasure of Bluebird Hall," Tad explained. "We've been looking for it, now and in the past, even though everybody said it didn't exist. And here it is, thanks to the owl and, I'm sure, thanks to Tamburlaine."

"Quick," interrupted Martha. "Let's see what it is."

Off came the wrappers.

"I was expecting jewels," Martha said, sighing.

"Or solid bricks of gold," said Tad.

"And all we get are books," said Joe, shaking his head. "What a life."

"Hey," said Martha. "I remember these. They're the

ones Granny Byram said her husband loved so much. She told us they were one of his greatest treasures, remember?"

"Sure I do," answered Tad. "But she didn't mean treasures like money, she meant treasures like something you care about."

"Well," said Martha, "I guess you're right, but they're nice to see again, anyway. If we can't have the regular kind of buried treasure, this kind isn't so bad after all."

"Yes," Tad agreed. "It reminds me of Granny Byram, and of John and of—"

"Did you say John?" asked Joe.

"Yes, why?"

"'Cause look," answered Joe. "I just found a piece of paper in one of these books, and it's signed John—and it's to the two of you."

"Let's see!" cried the twins. Looking together at the note in Joe's hands, they read:

Dear Tad, dear Martha,

Tamburlaine has explained much since your sudden disappearance so long ago. I am an old man now; and while I am still able to climb to the top of the house, I wanted to place these here for you.

Until we meet again.

John Byram
6th September, 1888

"How could someone who lived back then know you?" asked Joe, but Tad's mind was whirring so fast he didn't even hear the question.

"This has got to mean something," he said. "And there were books in those two pictures Great-aunt Ruth showed us!"

"Let's show them to Mom," Martha added, gently picking up the books. "Right this minute."

22

THANKSGIVING

"What is the meaning of this?" demanded Mr. Snivell, stomping one of his little feet on the hall carpet of Bluebird Hall. He was staring intently at a piece of paper Mrs. Byram had just given him.

"I think it's all perfectly clear," Mrs. Byram said, smiling. "Good day, Mr. Snivell. I'll thank you to leave my property immediately."

"B-but . . ." huffed Mr. Snivell. "I've brought my lawyer with me, and everything was sup—"

"Tad, Martha, Joe," said Mrs. Byram in a polite voice, "will you be good enough to show Mr. Snivell and his lawyer to the door?"

"You bet, Mom," said Joe.

Tad, Martha, and Joe soon found their places at the door. Joe was holding it wide open, Tad was giving a deep bow, and Martha was bending in a dramatic curtsey as Mr. Snivell passed through. He was still clutching the paper and fuming.

"You haven't seen the last of me—" he was saying

when, on the top step of Bluebird Hall, he encountered a just arrived Great-aunt Ruth.

"More's the pity," she said sweetly, stepping aside to allow Mr. Snivell to descend the four stairs to the front walk.

Was it a mistake, or did Great-aunt Ruth purposefully stick out her cane ever so slightly, causing Mr. Snivell to trip? With a curse and a howl, Mr. Snivell landed with a thud at the bottom of the stairs.

Looking up at the door, he could hear Great-aunt Ruth saying, "My, what a clumsy man!"

Then the door shut firmly on Mr. Snivell.

Events had happened very quickly after they showed their mother the books. Arching an eyebrow but saying nothing, she withdrew to the study. Following her, they found her scanning the bookshelves and at last pulling down a thick volume.

"Your father had some interest in rare books," she explained, glancing through the book's index. "This is a guide to collecting them."

Mrs. Byram turned to a page near the middle of the book. Frowning a bit, she read a paragraph or two. Then she smiled. Then she looked carefully at the books they had found. Then she re-read the guide. Then she smiled again, even wider.

"Mom, what's up?" asked Tad.

"Just say your prayers," their mother had replied, picking up the phone.

The friend Mrs. Byram had called was able to put her

in touch with a reliable rare book dealer. "You have what?" they could hear him shout, even through the telephone.

"Just what I said I had," answered Mrs. Byram.

"Tell me where you live," the dealer then said, "and I'll be there before noon tomorrow, with a check in my hand. If you have what you say you have, you're a very lucky woman."

"I know," Mrs. Byram had said with a smile.

Sure enough, the dealer arrived before noon. A thin, earnest man, he lost all composure when he was allowed to examine the books. When he had finished looking at all twelve, he gave a low whistle and shook his head excitedly.

"Do you have any idea how much these are worth?" he demanded.

"As a matter of fact, Mr. Maltby, I do," Mrs. Byram told him. "At Tad's suggestion, I called the woman in charge of the Rock Ridge Historical Society; it seems my son had met her at some point. At any rate, she dropped by last night and was able to update what I had read in one of my late husband's books. She had some recent auction reports dealing with rare books, so that gave me a fair notion of these books' value."

"I am prepared to exceed the highest bid in any auction you could name," replied Mr. Maltby. "I know a collector who's been seeking these very books for years."

"Fine," Mrs. Byram had answered. "I, for one, know precisely what I'm going to do with the money."

* * *

As it turned out, they only had to sell seven of the books to Mr. Maltby. They really were worth that much money.

"This more than pays off our mortgage," Mrs. Byram had explained, "as well as gives us enough extra money not to worry. I see no need to be piggish about it all."

Two of the remaining books they donated to the Rock Ridge Historical Society, the other three they kept. "One for each of you," their mother told Tad, Martha, and Joe.

So pleased was Great-aunt Ruth at the news, she splurged and took a taxi to Bluebird Hall the following Monday. She said she wanted to be there to see Mr. Snivell's expression when he saw a photocopy of the check to the bank with which Mrs. Byram had paid off her mortgage.

With some of the extra money from the sale of the books, the Byrams decided to paint the dining room, which had been sorely in need of work for a long time.

So it was that when they sat down for Thanksgiving dinner on Thursday, the room fairly glowed around them. Inside the room, you could say the Byrams were glowing as well.

"Our home is really ours," said Mrs. Byram happily, "and we're all together to enjoy it."

With their heads bowed, and holding hands tightly all around, they were silent as Great-aunt Ruth said grace before the meal: "Dear Lord, we who are gathered around this table thank You for all our blessings—this wonderful meal we enjoy, when so many go hungry; this beautiful house to shelter us, when so many are homeless; our good health to delight in, when so many are ill; and the love we cherish, when so many feel unloved. Make us worthy of all You have given, and keep us grateful in the midst of so much."

Five happy Byrams then dug into the meal, although Tad and Martha couldn't help but feel a little sad at the thought of never seeing Tamburlaine again, even though they knew he was safe and well in his own time and place.

"I wouldn't worry, if I were you," Great-aunt Ruth said suddenly to Tad and Martha when Mrs. Byram and Joe were briefly out of the room, seeing about something in the kitchen.

"Worry about what?" asked Tad.

"It is like a very wise man said to me, back when I was a girl, and more recently, now that I am old. He said that people who find magic once often find it again."

"So that explains—" said Tad as Mrs. Byram returned with Joe, carrying a cake she had made in the shape of Bluebird Hall.

"Oh, Mom," said Martha. "This is the best Thanksgiving we've ever had!"

And it was.